He was haunting her. There was no other word for it.

No, that was wrong. Diego Saez was hunting her.

And now, for the first time in her life, she knew what it felt like to be a hunter's quarry. Diego Saez was relentless. He had her in his sights, and he intended to bring her down.

"Come," said Diego, and slid his hand under her elbow.

Portia jerked away violently. She was trembling with emotion. It was rage—she knew it was rage. Cold, icy rage that this man—this vile, arrogant man—was simply assuming that she would fall into his bed like a ripe peach, just because he wanted her to….

Julia James

BEDDED BY BLACKMAIL

Bedded by... *Blackmail*

Forced to bed...then to wed?

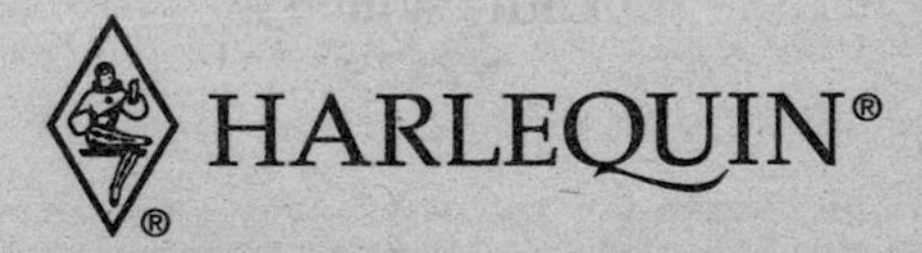

TORONTO • NEW YORK • LONDON
AMSTERDAM • PARIS • SYDNEY • HAMBURG
STOCKHOLM • ATHENS • TOKYO • MILAN • MADRID
PRAGUE • WARSAW • BUDAPEST • AUCKLAND

For my long-suffering, fabulously patient and, above all, inspiring editor, Kim—all my thanks for everything.

ISBN 0-373-12459-7

BEDDED BY BLACKMAIL

First North American Publication 2005.

This edition published by arrangement with Harlequin Books S.A.

www.eHarlequin.com

Printed in U.S.A.

CHAPTER ONE

'NOW, that one there. She interests me. Who is she?'

Diego Saez indicated with his wine glass before sweeping it back up to his lips to take another mouthful of the extremely expensive vintage wine. He lounged back in a stiff-backed chair, long legs extended under the damask-covered table. He looked relaxed, despite the formality of his evening dress. One hand lay on the tablecloth, the natural tan of his skin colour accentuated by the white linen. His dark, hooded eyes were very slightly narrowed, and his strong, compelling features held a considering expression.

The man beside him looked across the large, crowded dining hall. Stained glass windows pierced the outer wall, emblazoned with the arms of the City livery company where tonight's banking industry dinner was taking place. A wash of people, predominantly men, all attired in black-tie and evening dress, sat at the fifty or so tables filling the room. There was an aura of expensive wine, port and brandy, and faint fumes from cigars, for the Queen's toast had already been given so smoking was now permitted, as the several hundred guests relaxed for a while after dinner, before the evening's guest of honour—a senior politician—rose to give his speech.

'Which one?' asked the man sitting next to Diego Saez, craning his neck slightly to see where his companion was looking.

'The blonde in blue,' replied Diego laconically.

An unpleasant smile appeared briefly on the other man's narrow face.

'Not even you, Señor Saez, could do the business for

Portia Lanchester. And even if you did get up her skirt you'd just meet iron knickers!'

Diego took another mouthful of burgundy, savouring the bouquet a moment, and ignoring the comment. Its coarseness did not strike him as incongruous, merely repulsive. Upper class Englishmen might talk with plums in their mouths, but the sentiments they expressed—like that one—were by no means unusual amongst a certain type. And Piers Haddenham was definitely that type. His background might be moneyed, but his soul came from the gutter—and that was to insult the gutter. Diego had no illusions about him, or the rest of this collection of comfortably privileged company.

But then he had no illusions about anyone.

Especially women. They might play coy for a while, but they all came round in the end. Their reluctance never lasted long.

Diego's dark eyes narrowed again, studying the woman who had caught his attention.

He could only see her profile, but it was enough to tell him that he'd like to see the rest of her. She had those classic English rose looks—fair hair, translucent skin, and facial bones that told her bloodline as clearly as if she'd been a racehorse.

'Lanchester...' he murmured.

'Loring Lanchester,' supplied Haddenham.

'Ah, yes.' Diego nodded.

Loring Lanchester. Merchant bankers to Victorian industrialists and colonial expansionists. Now, a hundred and fifty years later, a complete anachronism. They should have been taken over by a global bank years ago if they were to have the slightest chance of long-term survival.

His razor-sharp mind worked rapidly, filing through the complicated landscape of the City's financial institutions, long since meshed into a global nexus that spanned the UK, Europe, America and the Pacific Ring like a spider's web. And one of the most skilful spiders, who could sense and exploit to his own unerring advantage every tremor in that delicate, complex web, was Diego Saez.

Quite who he was no one seemed to know. He was South American—but his Hispanic background, hinted at in the strong features was as far as anyone got in identifying him. Self-made; that much was evident. There was no Saez dynasty backing him, bankrolling him, opening doors for him. But then Diego Saez opened his own doors.

He'd opened them in New York, Sydney, Tokyo, Milan and Frankfurt, and any number of the less influential financial centres. Now he was busy opening them in London.

Not that he needed to exert any pressure. Doors opened magically for him the moment he expressed the slightest interest in any kind of venture or investment. His reputation as one of the most astute financiers operating on the global stage had gone before him. Saez made money. A lot of money.

Out of everything he touched.

And that made everyone—from chief executives to bankers, investment houses to industrialists—very, very keen to know what he was up to, and to get in on the act if they could.

Frustratingly, Diego Saez had a habit of keeping his cards close to his chest.

Piers Haddenham, despatched by his chairman to woo Saez during what seemed to be an impromptu visit to London, was doing his best to get a glimpse of those cards. But so far Diego Saez had done little more than make enticingly ambiguous remarks—possibly leading, more probably misleading—and sport a sardonic look in his eye whenever Piers tried to steer the conversation towards what might or might not be attracting his interest right now.

Apart from Portia Lanchester.

Piers looked at the woman again, this time with a different mindset. He'd assumed Saez was simply thinking of the night ahead, who he would warm his sheets with, but perhaps he was still running on his daytime agenda.

Loring Lanchester. Was that the name on one of the cards Saez was thinking of playing during his visit to the UK?

He decided to see if he could draw Saez out.

'Not in the best of health these days,' he observed. 'Old man Loring lost his marbles years ago, but won't give up the chairmanship. And young Tom Lanchester, the nephew, is even more useless.' He paused a moment. 'Took some reckless decisions recently, so I heard. Wouldn't like their asset book myself.'

He glanced at his dinner companion, to see whether his fishing line would twitch, but Diego Saez was merely looking bored, waiting for him to stop speaking.

'So...' mused Diego, flexing his legs slightly under the table—his chair was quite inadequate for his tall frame. 'Why the ironclad underwear?'

Piers's face relaxed. His initial assumption had been right after all. Saez was simply after sex. Not that he'd get any from Tom Lanchester's cold bitch of a sister. No one did. Certainly not that poor sod Simon Masters, who was sitting next to her and just about panting. Piers didn't know anyone who'd got their leg over Portia Lanchester.

His brow furrowed momentarily. Hadn't she been engaged once? A few years back? Who the hell had volunteered to get his tackle frozen in that glacier? He'd bolted, anyway, whoever he was, and married someone else, and since then her name never came up when the brandy came out—well, not unless the subject was ice maidens.

Not even Diego Saez could heat her up, thought Piers dismissively. Not that he didn't roll an enviable number of women, but none of the ones he'd ever been seen with could have been described as cold. Hot ones, yes, like that Latino singer—Diana Someone—and the Italian opera diva, Cristina Something. Plus a French countess, a Moroccan model and a Hungarian tennis ace. And that had just been this year. A sour look, of male envy, lit his eye.

Women fell over themselves to drool—and drop their knickers.

The sour look vanished. Malice gleamed briefly. No way would Portia Lanchester go for Saez.

He leant towards Diego and said confidingly, 'Frigid, that's why. Listen—' he slid his hand inside his tuxedo and drew out a card that looked like an ordinary business card '—don't waste your time on her. Phone this number and you'll have someone waiting for you in your hotel suite. Tell them your spec and they'll deliver whatever you want—and your choice of equipment.' He proffered the card to Diego. 'They're all clean—I use them myself. And they take credit cards, of course.'

Diego drew his arm away and suppressed an instinct to slam his fist into Haddenham's corrupt, narrow face. Instead, he drained the last of his wine and reached for the port bottle, which had stopped its circulation conveniently to hand. He decanted a generous measure into the appropriate glass.

'I believe we are about to suffer for our supper,' he remarked, looking towards the top table, where the scarlet-coated Master of Ceremonies was stepping forward, gavel at the ready, to call for silence—and then the dreaded speeches.

Diego lifted his port glass and prepared to be bored, instead of revolted.

Then, as the politician was introduced and stood up to give his prepared speech on the state of the UK economy, his eyes drifted back to where Portia Lanchester was sitting. Ramrod-straight, her well-bred chin lifted, she displayed no emotion on her fine-boned, aristocratic face.

Diego sat back again and wondered what she looked like naked.

He had every intention of finding out.

* * *

Portia sat motionless, hands in her lap, her face blank to conceal her acute boredom, as the speaker droned on, immensely pleased with the sound of his own voice.

But then the whole evening had been exquisitely tedious. God alone knew why she had given in to Simon's endless cajolings to come along as his partner. She'd done it out of a combination of exasperation and pity. Simon kept thinking that if only he didn't give in she would take him seriously. His dogged determination to woo her both irritated and softened her. Though she would never be stupid enough to go out with him on a real date, lest he get hopeless hopes up, tonight's stuffy City do, with wall-to-wall bankers, had seemed innocuous enough.

She hadn't realised just how incredibly dreadful it would be. Money and politics dominated the conversation, and she was interested in neither. She was also the only woman on her table—one of little more than a few dozen women in the whole room—and as the wine had gone down so the awareness of the several hundred men in the room to the presence of any females at all had increased accordingly. She had begun to be on the receiving end of some very open assessment—something she had always loathed.

She had reacted by adopting her usual defence—total and deliberate freezing. By refusing to acknowledge how they were looking her over she could pretend they were not. Simon's presence did not seem to deter them sufficiently—but then he was not particularly put out by the attention she was getting. Irritatedly she knew that he was actually enjoying having his escort lusted after—it made him feel envied, and he presumably liked the idea of that.

Suppressing a sigh, half of annoyance, half of boredom, she reached out and took a sip of mineral water from her glass, then idly nibbled at a *petit-four* from the plate in front of her. The politician droned on, talking about interest rates and invisible earnings and fiscal instruments, none of which she had the slightest interest in.

Poor Tom. She thought instinctively of her brother. He

has to know all this stuff. Not that he liked it either. But the wretched bank needed him, so he had to put up with all this boring finance-speak. At least he was escaping this shindig tonight—from the looks of him he was coming down with flu, and he was keeping indoors. She didn't blame him.

She stared into the distance and let her mind drift away to something she *was* interested in—producing a definitive catalogue of the Regency portraitist Benjamin Teller. She still needed to trace several missing paintings—plus *Mr Orde with Gun Dog, 1816* was proving tricky to attribute conclusively. And she still needed to identify the woman portrayed in the *Young Lady with Harp, 1809*. She was pretty sure she was Miss Maria Colding, of Harthwaite, Yorkshire, but needed proof. She would have to visit Harthwaite, she suspected, and check out what other family portraits were still hanging there, then sift through the county archives to see if there was a commissioning letter or bill of payment still in existence.

Finally the speech concluded and the politician resumed his seat to polite applause.

Talk broke out again at her table, and Simon leant across, patting her hand.

'Phew, what a number! Were you completely bored?'

He sounded so anxious she hadn't the heart to agree too acidly.

'Does anyone actually listen to these things?' she asked, putting a slight smile on her mouth.

'Lord, no. Well, only the hacks on the press table, I suppose. They'll pounce on anything they can turn into a headline.'

She reached for her water again, and took another, longer drink.

'Are you up for a liqueur now?' her escort asked attentively.

She shook her head. The last thing she wanted was any more alcohol. She'd drunk champagne at the reception, then both white and red wine over dinner.

'Coffee would be lovely. Is there any left in that pot there?'

Simon immediately reached across to where the silver coffee pot hid behind the flower arrangement in the centre of the table. Portia slid her cup towards him. The back of her neck was stiff. It must be the effort of holding still for so long during that speech. Gracefully she twisted her head to the left, and then to the right, to ease the stiffness.

And froze.

A man was looking at her.

Correction. A man was looking her over. His hooded eyes were resting on her with lazy assessment.

Something like a hot thread of wire drew through her stomach.

As if in total slow motion she felt her pupils dilate.

She stared, unable to move her gaze away.

He was sitting a few tables away, right in her eyeline through the mesh of heads and bodies at the other tables in between. He was tall; she could tell that even with him sitting back, lounged in his seat. His skin was dark for a European, but with a deep, natural tan. Mediterranean? Not quite. Too big to be Italian or Greek, anyway. High cheekbones. Strong nose. Deep lines running to the edges of his mouth. Eyes dark. Very dark.

And still looking her over.

As her eyes met his, she felt the hot wire draw out through her spine.

Liquefying it.

For one endless moment she could not move, and then, with an effort of will that made her weak, she averted her face.

'Cream?'

She jumped minutely, forcing her eyes to focus on the cream jug held in Simon's hand over the cup of coffee he'd just poured her.

'No, thanks.'

Did her voice sound different? Shaky?

She reached for the cup and lifted it to her lips. The caffeine jolted her, and she was grateful. As she sipped, she recovered her composure.

Oh, for heaven's sake, she snapped to herself—he just took you by surprise, that's all.

Usually she was careful never to make eye contact when a man looked at her in that way. She'd just been caught off guard this time. That was all. A mistake, and one she must ensure she would not repeat. She schooled a look of blankness to her face, the one she usually fielded to members of the male population unless she knew she could trust them.

She drank more coffee, trying to listen to whatever Simon was saying to her.

But she felt uncomfortable still. Her nape was prickling now—and she knew why.

Unbidden, his face leapt in her mental vision again—those strong features, that expression of cynicism mixed with an open sexual appraisal.

The wire began to pull slowly through her again.

Stop this!

Her mind snapped away, concentrating on Simon. He was a nice enough escort, and certainly never pushed his luck with her or tried it on. She was easy enough with him, in a casually indifferent way. He didn't threaten her.

Not like the man watching her…

Now that that the wretched speech was finally over, surely she could get away? She would finish her coffee and then get Simon to put her into a taxi. She wouldn't let him come with her—he would probably get desperate and try to pounce, and she didn't want that. She liked him, and didn't want to hurt him. Better by far to end the evening in public and escape on her own.

She wondered if Tom would still be up. She hoped not. He needed an early night. He hadn't looked well at all.

A faint furrow of concern marked her brow. Was it just flu? He'd seemed under the weather for a good few months now. She hadn't seen a great deal of him recently—she'd been off in the States last month, tracking down some of the Tellers that had got sold to American buyers years ago. He ought to get out of London, spend some time at Salton. Catch up with Felicity.

They really ought to get on with it and marry, Portia found herself thinking—a familiar refrain. They were so obviously ideal for each other. Neither liked London, and both were far happier at Salton. Felicity would be ideal for Salton, Portia knew. She had an instinctive feel for the place. She wouldn't muck it up. She'd leave things alone.

Portia had lived in dread that Tom would marry some woman who would summon an army of ghastly fashionable interior designers and turn Salton into some vile 'showpiece'—but Felicity Pethridge would never do that. She'd just settle in, be devoted to Tom, give him a brood of tumbling children, and take her place as one of the long, long line of châtelaines who had kept Salton going through the centuries.

A poignant look softened Portia's clear grey eyes. It was one of the painful ironies of the English land inheritance system that daughters never got to live in the houses they grew up in—not unless there was no son to inherit, of course. Daughters had to go off and look after someone else's place. A guilty look entered her eye. That had been the main appeal of Geoffrey Chandler, she knew—not him, but the prospect of running his vast Elizabethan pile in Shropshire, which came complete with an art collection.

But although the art collection had been to die for, it hadn't proved sufficient to marry for. Poor Geoffrey. If he hadn't managed to persuade her—against her better judgement—to pre-empt their wedding night, she might have gone ahead and married him. As it was, a month in Tuscany with him had made her realise she couldn't possibly go ahead with the wedding. Not even holing up in the Uffizi for sanctuary during the day had been compensation for the ordeals of the night.

Instinctively her mind shied away from the memories. He'd tried so *hard*, and she'd still hated it. And even though she'd tried desperately not to let her revulsion show, of course he had realised—and that had just made things even more unbearable.

Ending the engagement had been awful too—painful and embarrassing, and making her feel so guilty. And when Geoffrey had announced a whirlwind engagement to one of her own schoolfriends not two months later she'd felt more than guilty.

She'd felt totally inadequate.

A shiver went through her. After the disaster with poor Geoffrey she'd simply given up on sex, and had found abstinence a huge relief. She knew that the men of her acquaintance thought her frigid, but she didn't care. She just wanted them to leave her alone.

She didn't even like them looking at her.

The nape of her neck prickled again. That wretched man was still over there, keeping his eyes on her.

Dark, hooded eyes…

She straightened her back and pushed her coffee cup away. For one extraordinary, inexplicable moment she'd wanted to turn her head and check whether he was, indeed, still keeping her in his eyeline.

Instead, she turned to Simon.

'I don't mean to be a wet blanket, Si, but I've got quite an early start tomorrow. Do you think you could get me a cab? I'd better make a move.'

Disappointment showed in his pale blue eyes.

'Must you? I thought we might be able to take in a club...'

He sounded so hopeful she hated to turn him down. But what was the point of going on anywhere with him? He'd just get ideas. Hopes.

She laid a hand on his sleeve. 'I don't think so, Simon—I'm sorry.'

There had been pity in her eyes, and she saw him flinch and hated herself for it.

She got to her feet, and the rest of the men at the table, realising she was leaving, stood up as well. She took her leave, bidding them all goodnight, and one of the younger ones asked her to give his regards to Tom.

'No show tonight, I see,' the man said. 'Well, it's understandable.'

'He's got flu,' said Portia.

Another of the men laughed. 'He's certainly caught a cold, all right!'

The others laughed, exchanging glances. Portia frowned. She hadn't a clue what they meant, and didn't want to know. She just wanted to head for home.

She bent down to retrieve her evening bag from under her chair and stood away from the table. Simon took her arm and they started to make their way to the exit, on the far side of the room. With the speeches over there was a lot of movement, with people heading out to the restrooms or to the bar in the reception lobby, or just to go and catch up with diners at other tables.

As she made her way on Simon's arm several people stopped to greet him and chat innocuously. Dutifully she paused, making whatever responses were called for. Their progress was slow, however, and at one point she realised they had become stalled just beside the table occupied by the man she had intercepted looking her over. A faint prickle of unease went through her and she felt herself tensing, then becoming irritated by her own reaction. She risked a brief glance towards the table.

His place was empty, and she felt an irrational spurt of relief. Then, as her eyes swept back to Simon, engaged in conversation with a man who appeared to be a former colleague at another brokers, she stiffened abruptly.

He was talking to two other men. One was slightly built, with a narrow, fox-like face she didn't like. The other was in his sixties, portly, smoking a cigar and red-faced. She heard the narrow-faced man call him 'Sir Edward' in obsequious tones.

The man who had been looking her over said something. It was deep and laconic, with an accent that sounded more American than anything else, though there was definitely something foreign about it. English, even American English, was not his first language, she guessed.

He was tall, all right. Easily over six feet, with broad shoulders. He made the narrow-faced man look like an unhealthy weasel, and the older man like an overweight bear.

But then, Portia found herself thinking, he would make any man look disadvantaged.

For all his height, and breadth of shoulder, there was an innate grace about him. As if his body were under perfect control.

It was certainly in good shape, that was for sure. His torso was lean, his legs long and muscled...she could see how the material of his dinner suit was pulled taut over his thighs.

What on earth am I doing? she suddenly thought. She tried to drag her eyes away, but they swept over his face as she did so. She wished they hadn't, because all over again it had the same impact on her as it had before. The deep, curving lines from his nose to his mouth drew her eyes, the high cheekbones, the plane of his jaw. Those hooded eyes...

Suddenly, and without warning, his eyes flickered to hers.

The hot wire jerked through her.

For one long, unbearable moment he held her gaze.

Heat flushed her skin, and she was suddenly vividly aware of her bare arms and shoulders. Even though her dark blue evening dress was not in the least décolleté she suddenly felt hideously, horribly exposed.

She wanted a shawl, a wrap—a blanket!—anything to cover herself up under that gaze.

But she had nothing. Nothing to conceal herself with.

Automatically, unconsciously, her chin went up and she looked away, back to Simon.

Three feet away from her, Diego Saez smiled.

Seducing Portia Lanchester was clearly going to be an amusing enterprise.

And different, very different, from his usual affairs.

Typically, the women he selected for his bed required nothing more than an indication on his part that he found them desirable. His problem was getting rid of them, not getting them in the first place.

Not that he envisaged any serious problem with Portia Lanchester.

Her reaction to him demonstrated that amply. She was aware of him, all right, and that was the first step of the journey for her. The journey that would end in his bed.

Not tonight, however. There was no point hurrying her. He wanted to take his time over this one. Enjoy every stage of the seduction. By midday tomorrow he'd have a complete dossier on her, courtesy of his security agency, and then he'd take it from there. For now, he would just enjoy continuing to make her aware of him.

He flicked his attention back to what Sir Edward Porter, a former but still influential chairman of a major bank, was saying about the current level of merger and acquisition activity in the City, and made some appropriate comment.

With more animation that she was feeling, Portia joined in the chit-chat with Simon and the other man. Then, as she recovered her composure, she decided enough was enough. Taking ruthless advantage of a momentary pause, she spoke up.

'Simon—my cab?' she prompted.

Reluctantly he moved off, or tried to, but suddenly, and she didn't quite see how, her way was blocked. The trio ahead of her seemed to have shifted somehow, and now the man who'd been looking her over was right in her path.

'Excuse me.'

Her tone was clipped.

For a moment he did not move. She levelled her gaze at him—though it meant looking up at him.

The dark eyes swept over her face one last time, and for one last time she felt that hot wire jerk.

Her lips pressed together. Anger spurted through her. She moved to step around him, and then immediately he had stepped away, clearing the way for her.

'Thank you,' she said, her voice even more clipped, simultaneously dropping her eyes. She marched forward, still angry.

Behind her, Simon hurried to catch up.

Diego let his gaze linger on her receding form for a few more seconds, then cut back to Sir Edward.

'Loring Lanchester...' he said speculatively. 'Are they as vulnerable as they look, do you think?'

At his side, Piers Haddenham's eyes gleamed. So, not sex after all, then. He listened with acute attention to Sir Edward's reply.

'Sinking faster than the *Titanic*,' the older man said succinctly. 'Unless they get a tow—and by a pretty damn large ship!' His shrewd eyes met Diego's speculatively.

Diego's expression did not change.

Far across the room, he could see the elegant, slender form of Portia Lanchester walking out.

CHAPTER TWO

'NEXT Thursday at two? That would be wonderful. Thank you so much!'

Portia put the phone down. Descendants of the Coldings still lived at Hathwaite, and were happy for her to inspect their remaining portraits and compare them with the photos she'd taken of the mysterious *Young Lady with Harp*. Their family papers had been deposited with the county records archive years ago, and she would do a search through them the following day if her suspicions about Miss Maria Colding proved well-founded. With a feeling of satisfaction she tidied the papers on her desk.

Her work at a small but prestigious art history research institute never failed to fascinate her. She knew she was very fortunate to have been taken on, though she was also well aware that the institute director, Hugh Mackerras, considered it a definite plus that she possessed an ample private income of her own. It meant not only that he could pay her very modestly indeed, but that she was more than ready to fund her own travel expenses. But she was pleased to do so—she knew she was fortunate not to be financially dependent on her salary, which meant she was able to pursue a career that really interested her, rather than one that kept body and soul together.

A slight pang of guilt assailed her. She enjoyed her substantial private income thanks to Loring Lanchester—and it was thanks to poor Tom, incarcerated there, that the family merchant bank kept going. Poor Tom. He really wasn't cut out to be a banker—he was much happier tramping through fields in his gumboots and Barbar, getting stuck in to the muddy side of agriculture.

Thinking of Tom made her remember that awful dinner the night before—and that brought another memory in tow.

A shiver went through her.

That wretched man had disturbed her, whether she wanted to admit it or not. There had been something about him that had seemed to threaten her.

In her mind's eye she saw him again, lounging back in his chair, cradling his wine glass, his hooded eyes resting on her, looking at her.

Even as it had last night, she felt her skin begin to prickle.

With a shake of annoyance at such a ridiculous over-reaction to a man whose name she did not even know she returned her attention to her notes. As she did so she realised she was suppressing a slight yawn. She was not surprised. She had not had a good night. The wine had made her sleepy, but although she'd slept as soon as her head hit the pillow, she'd had dreams she wished she hadn't.

Dark, intent eyes had haunted her dreams.

Dreams of being watched, assessed.

Desired.

The phone rang, jolting her out of an unpleasant train of thought.

She lifted the receiver and cleared her mind.

'Yes?' Her voice was crisp and businesslike.

'May I speak to Portia Lanchester?'

She stilled disbelievingly. The voice at the other end of the phone was deep, with a distinct foreign accent, plus echoes of American. The line was distorting the voice, changing the balance of the mingled accents, but she recognised it.

Think of the devil and he'll come calling…

The words leapt in her mind and she pushed them aside. For a second only she paused, getting back her composure.

'Speaking,' she answered. The breath seemed tight in her chest.

'Miss Lanchester? My name is Diego Saez—I noticed you last night at the dinner. Are you free for lunch today?'

Her chest tightened even more.

'I beg your pardon?'

Her voice chilled the line.

'Are you free for lunch?' he repeated. She heard a trace of amusement in his voice, as if her answer had been predictable.

For the briefest second she paused, then, in crystal-cut accents she said succinctly, 'I'm afraid not.'

She put the phone down.

Her heart, she realised, seemed to be beating most unevenly.

She'd been rude, she knew she had, but she excused herself. She had just wanted to get him off the line.

Urgently. Instinctively.

Slowly, deliberately, she let the breath out of her lungs. Her eyes rested on the phone. She wondered if it was going to ring again. But it stayed silent.

Diego Saez.

So that was what his name was.

Her mind ran automatically. Spanish—or Hispanic at any rate. South American? Latino?

How did he know my name? My work number?

She pursed her lips. It didn't matter how he knew, he wasn't going to get anywhere with her.

Why not?

The question slid into her brain like a stiletto knifeblade. In answer, her lips pursed even more. Why not? What kind of question was that? The man had eyed her up like a slab of meat and she had to ask Why not? about him?

Angrily, she flicked through the papers on her desk, looking for the one she wanted. She found it and started to read. Within minutes she was back in the world of early-nineteenth-century portraiture.

Two hours later a massive bouquet of flowers arrived—exotic scented lilies and tropical ferns. The accompanying card simply said 'D.S.' on it. She fetched a vase from the kitchen in the basement of the old Georgian house in Bloomsbury that housed the institute and plunged the flowers into water. Their scent filled her small office—rich and overpowering.

As she left the institute that evening she took the vase downstairs with her, and left it in Reception. She didn't want it in her office.

The scent disturbed her.

A mile or two west of Bloomsbury, Diego Saez glanced at the ticket that had just been couriered to his hotel suite. It lay on the glass coffee table in the suite's lounge, next to a freshly typed dossier that had been delivered before noon that day. It outlined in considerable detail a great deal of personal information about the individual who was the subject of investigation. Although Diego had been in meetings all day he'd had time to peruse it and take action accordingly.

He had the main facts that he required, from her age—twenty-five—to her employer, her home address, family connections and key friends, and social interests.

That Portia Lanchester had not jumped at his invitation to lunch neither surprised nor bothered him. On the contrary, it pleased him. Had she proved, like other women, to be eager for his attentions after all, she would have already started to bore him.

A leisurely pursuit of her would be far more enjoyable.

He gave a slight, self-mocking smile. Even if it meant enduring an evening spent in surroundings even less congenial than last night's City dinner. Still, the evening would have its compensations.

He strolled off to his bedroom, ready to shower and change.

Portia eased her way through the crush of people in the foyer, following her old schoolfriend Susie Winterton and her mother as they crowded into the auditorium. The two-minute bell was sounding and she wanted to get to her seat. In the pit the orchestra was already tuning up, and she glanced around at the familiar red and gold glory of the Royal Opera House, Covent Garden. A sense of pleasant anticipation filled her. *La Traviata* was one of her favourite operas. But as she reached their row in the front stalls, and started to thread her way along it, her sense of pleasant anticipation drained away totally, replaced by cold shock.

Diego Saez had the seat next to her.

He stood up as she took her place.

'Miss Lanchester,' he said politely. His eyes were mockingly amused.

On her other side, Susie, leaning forward, said brightly, 'Oh, do you two know each other?' Her eyes gleamed with curiosity.

'No,' said Portia tightly, and opened her programme.

'We met the other evening,' he contradicted, and bestowed a smile on Susie. She, treacherously, reacted predictably and returned the smile with an openly questioning look on her round face.

'Diego Saez—' He held out his hand.

There were introductions all round, and a lot of speculative looks cast by Susie at Portia. Portia continued to bury her head in her programme as much as she could, uttering the barest monosyllables as Susie chattered away to the man she obviously found fascinatingly masculine. The arrival of the conductor and the dimming of the house lights as the overture started was a blessed reprieve.

But throughout the performance Portia was punishingly aware of the tall, dark frame beside her. He seemed to intrude into her personal space, though his long legs were slanted away from her, and not even the sleeve of his tuxedo touched her arm. But it was more than her body space that seemed threatened—it was her mental space too.

She was aware of him. Horribly, inextricably aware of

him. She could feel him beside her, inhale the scent that had to be him—a mix of subtle, faintly spiced aftershave and his own masculinity. She wanted to pull away from him, but wouldn't. But as the evening wore on awareness sharpened into hyper-awareness. The second interval was even worse than the first had been.

In the first, Portia had at least had the company of Susie and her mother. Diego Saez had managed to take over, somehow, though she hadn't the faintest idea how he'd done it. He'd simply ushered them all along to the bar and sorted drinks for them in an instant. Then he'd stayed, chatting courteously to Susie and her mother, hardly saying a word to Portia. Not even looking at her. He had smiled down at Susie, and Portia's lips had thinned as she sipped her gin and tonic. Susie had chattered away like an idiot, and her mother had smiled benignly, clearly equally impressed by this imposing, attentive male.

But now, in the second interval, Susie proved even more treacherous. As they took their drinks, she suddenly squealed, 'Oh, look, there's Fiona and Andrew—*do* let's say hello!' She dragged her mother across to the other couple, pointedly deserting Portia.

Diego Saez glanced down at her.

Her lips tightened, fingers pressing on the stem of the glass holding gently fizzing mineral water—a second gin and tonic would be unwise, she knew. She steeled herself. He was probably going to try and invite her out again, suggest post-theatre dinner, or make some reference to the flowers he'd sent, or explain how he'd managed to find out she'd be here tonight and get the seat next to her. She instinctively knew—accident it had *not* been!

But he did none of those things. To her stunned disbelief, she felt his fingers stroke along the nape of her neck.

'I'm told,' said Diego Saez, in a low, considering voice, 'that you're frigid. Is that so?' His fingers moved on her skin, then stilled, feeling the instant trembling, quivering reaction to his touch, and rested. 'No, I think not,' he drawled, and dropped his hand away.

She couldn't move. Not a muscle. Her anger was so great that for a second she thought she would not be able to stop her arm swinging up and her palm swiping right across his face.

Something moved in his eyes.

It was amusement.

'Try it,' he murmured. 'It should go down well in a place like this.'

She turned on her heel, but in that instant her wrist was caught and held. 'Sometimes,' he told her, his voice quiet, 'a delicate courtship is…inappropriate.'

He let her go. Then abruptly he walked away, heading for the foyer. She stood watching him, staring blindly, anger washing in icy waves through her.

And something else. Something she wouldn't think about.

Wouldn't.

For the rest of the evening her stomach churned, as if she had swallowed live worms. It was a horrible feeling.

There was only one source of relief. Diego Saez had left before the final act. Portia could only be grovellingly grateful—though her gratitude was severely curtailed by the fact that his absence only meant that Susie felt free to interrogate her thoroughly in low, excited tones, all the way out to the taxi at the end of the opera.

'Portia!' Susie gripped her arm. 'He's gorgeous! *So* sexy!' She spoke in a low voice, so her mother wouldn't hear. 'I'm going to phone you tomorrow and you've got to tell me *all* about him!'

Portia eyed her balefully. 'There is nothing to tell. Susie, please don't make anything out of this. I don't intend to have anything to do with the man.'

Her friend stared at her.

'You're mad,' she said roundly. 'Completely loopy.

Anyway—' she glanced sideways at Portia '—I don't think it's really going to matter what you intend or not. He doesn't look like a man who's used to being turned down.'

'Well, he'd better *start* getting used to it!' Portia snapped.

CHAPTER THREE

HE WAS haunting her. There was no other word for it.

No, that was wrong. Diego Saez was *hunting* her.

Portia had never felt strongly one way or the other about blood sports. She'd grown up with them, as part of country life, but, being arty rather than horsy, had never hunted.

But now, for the first time in her life, she knew what it felt like to be a hunter's quarry.

Diego Saez was relentless. He had her in his sights and he intended to bring her down. Other men had pursued her in her time, but none like this. Others she had frozen off and eventually they'd given up. Anyway, since Geoffrey she'd stuck to totally safe men, like Simon and a couple of Tom's friends, if she ever needed an escort anywhere or simply a partner for a dinner party and so on. But she made sure it was understood by any man who accompanied her that sex was not on the menu.

When it came to Diego Saez it was perfectly, glaringly obvious that sex was the only thing on the menu. A man like that wasn't going to exercise the slightest self-restraint.

She pressed her lips together. Why the hell couldn't he go and get sex from someone else, in that case? Good grief, it hadn't taken her long to be informed by a blatantly fascinated Susie that most women were only too keen to get his attention in that way. Not only was he *fabulously* rich, and *exotically* South American, he also, Susie confided avidly, when she turned up the next day to drag Portia out to lunch, had a reputation for flaunting one fantastic-looking female after another.

'Bully for him,' Portia answered tartly.

'You should be flattered he's keen on you,' Susie reprimanded her reproachfully. 'I mean, compared with Simon Masters the man is just sex on legs! He's as rich as anything, and I mean, *look* at him! Simon's totally wet in comparison!'

'Simon's very sweet!' Portia retorted.

Susie groaned derisively. 'Oh, *sweet*—you don't want *sweet* in bed. You want someone like Diego Saez. He just *drips* sex!' She gave a delicious shiver. 'God, Portia, even you must feel it!'

Portia speared a green bean viciously on her plate. Feel it?

Her fingers gripped her fork. Oh, yes, she felt it all right.

She felt those hooded eyes on her, appraising her—waiting for her.

Waiting for her to give in to him. To let those long, skilful fingers brush across her bare skin, as they had already done so devastatingly last night at the opera. He had touched her for only a few moments, but it had been enough—enough to make her realise how very, very dangerous Diego Saez was to her.

Her anger at his insolence—touching her, *daring* to ask her if she was frigid. Daring to make such a personal, intimate comment to her—had been a relief.

A refuge.

She worked hard to keep her anger at him going. She had to. Had to keep it as her primary response to him when she encountered him—yet again—wherever she seemed to go.

Suddenly, out of nowhere, it seemed, Diego Saez had developed an interest in being an art patron. The London art world was delighted—Diego Saez was too rich for them not to be eager for his interest.

She started seeing him everywhere—at private views, art auctions, sponsors' events and even, worst of all, at private parties. To find him intruding into her own social circuit appalled her, but how could she tell a hostess that if her latest guest was the rich and magnetically attractive South

American financier Diego Saez then she, Portia Lanchester, unspectacular art historian, would decline the invitation?

It didn't matter that he never invited her out again, never even singled her out for conversation. He was just there—everywhere. She couldn't escape him.

He was like a hair shirt, she thought. Her own personal hair shirt—mortifying her flesh. Making her, with every amused, taunting glance, punishingly aware of her own physicality. His considering appraisal of her—never overt enough to draw the attention of others, but always there, never turned off, even when he wasn't looking directly at her—made her hypersensitive to her own body. She saw the graceful twist of her wrists as she ate, felt the movement of her head on her slender neck as she turned to talk to someone, felt the brush of her dress against her breasts, the press of her thighs, one against the other…

It was a constant torment, making her feel like this.

How could he do this to her? How could he make her so aware of herself? And worse, much worse, aware of him?

Aware of the way his dark, knowing, heavy-lidded eyes would rest on her, aware of the strong width of his shoulders, the lean, hard-packed lines of his body. The sensual twist of his mouth.

She'd never been so aware of a man in her life. And she didn't want to be aware of him—didn't want to feel this panicky, jittery rushing of blood through her veins whenever she saw him, didn't want to feel the heat flushing through her skin when she realised he was, yet again, looking at her.

Why couldn't she control her reaction to him? Why—she shut her eyes in despair—was she reacting to him in the first place?

He was the *last* kind of man she should want to have any interest in! Too rich, too arrogant, too blatant, too—too everything. She hated that type! The type that thought they owned the world and could help themselves to anything in it.

Including all the women they wanted.

And she knew exactly how long he'd keep a woman—a handful of weeks, a month or two at the most. During their brief affair his mistress would be seen everywhere with him, at one glittering event after another, his 'constant companion' as the coy vulgarity of the tabloids loved to put it, and then, when he was bored—dumped. The end. *Nada.*

And he'd be on to the next one.

She'd got a rundown from Susie—uninvited, but that hadn't stopped her friend from telling her—on just how many women he'd been seen around with in Europe and America in the last year alone. There'd been an opera singer, a model and a tennis ace, just for starters.

All of them had been glamorous, high-profile and astonishingly beautiful women, with fantastic figures and dramatic personalities.

So why is he the slightest bit interested in *me*? Portia thought bitterly.

Susie echoed her question, but from a quite different angle.

'Honestly, Portia, you should be flattered he's keen on you! He can pick and choose, you know!'

'Well, let him pick and choose someone else, then!' Portia replied tightly.

Susie looked at her.

'You know, it would do you good to let him have his wicked way with you.'

Portia stared disbelievingly at her friend.

'What?'

'I mean it,' said Susie doggedly. 'You need a man, Portia. You haven't been out with anyone since you and Geoffrey split up.'

Portia's face had gone rigid. 'I've been out with Simon Masters—'

Susie interrupted her ruthlessly. 'I mean a real man, not a wet rag! This Diego Saez would be ideal for you!'

'*Ideal?* Are you insane?'

'No, just realistic. Look, I know you were cut up over Geoffrey, but you can't just shut yourself away for the rest of your life. It's ridiculous! That's why someone like Diego Saez would be so good for you. Boy, would he get you cured!'

Portia's mouth tightened.

'Thank you—but I don't consider myself to be in need of a cure.'

'Just a good, *hard* man—excuse the expression, but it's true. Someone who'll sweep away all those inhibitions and let you rejoin the female sex!'

Portia turned on her icily.

'Believe me, Susie, *when* I "rejoin the female sex," as you so charmingly put it, it will *not* be with some ruthless Latin Lothario like Diego Saez!'

Susie was unrepentant.

'Why not?'

'Why not? Are you mad? Do you seriously think any intelligent woman would want to humiliate herself like that? Be the latest idiotic *floozy* for Diego Saez to amuse himself with, and then get dumped two weeks later when he goes on to his next glorious conquest? And have everyone laugh at her when he'd dumped her?'

She shuddered.

Susie just laughed. 'Oh, don't be so negative! Think of the fun you'd have for a fortnight. And anyway—who knows?—Diego Saez might fall headlong in love with your blonde English looks, sweep you off to his million-acre ranch in Argentina and keep you in polo ponies for the rest of your life!'

'Very amusing,' Portia answered humourlessly.

She could see no humour in the situation at all. Susie didn't know what it was like. She thought it would be *fun* to have someone like Diego Saez pursue you. Fun? *Fun* to have his dark, heavy-lidded eyes seek you out across a room, make you feel, suddenly and shamingly, as if you were in your underwear, or, worse, make you stall halfway through a sentence and find the breath tight in your throat. *Fun* to know that of all the men in the world none had *ever* made her react like this.

It was terrifying, mortifying.

She didn't *want* to react to a man like Diego Saez. So why, *why* did she have to be so punishingly, *stupidly* aware of him the whole time? Why couldn't she just ignore him?

She did her best. Did her best to put him off her.

If she couldn't avoid him—and it seemed she couldn't, so intrusive was he everywhere she went—then she could at least try and make herself as inconspicuous as possible. As undesirable.

She tried concealing her body. At the next private view she went to she wore a dress that had a high, Chinese-style collar, long sleeves down to the backs of her hands and a hem down to her ankle, with flat slippers that did not lift her hips.

When her tormentor arrived, fussed over by everyone there, he let his glance rest momentarily on Portia, who lifted her chin and looked right through him—but not sufficiently to miss the mocking twist of his mouth as he took in her suppressed appearance.

When the opportunity came he strolled across to her.

'Very erotic,' he murmured. 'You must wear it for me some time—privately.'

Then, before she could say a word, he strolled off again. A redhead, poured into a clinging emerald-green cocktail dress, seized his arm and pressed herself against him blatantly, making it clear how attractive she found him.

Portia glared after him, rigid with fury.

And something even worse.

The jittery, panicky feeling filled her again, and to her disgust she found that she was watching him, seeing how he smiled down at the redhead, who was rubbing up against him now, his mouth giving that sensual twist that disturbed her so much.

She felt that hot wire tug inside her, and forcibly turned her head away so she could not see him.

Why? she thought despairingly. Why was he getting to her like this?

Why couldn't he just clear out? Go back to Wall Street, Geneva, Buenos Aires—wherever he came from!

And leave her alone.

That was all she wanted. Just to be left alone.

She got some relief when Susie reported—reproachfully—that he had started being seen around with a well-known actress currently starring in a West End hit.

'Good,' said Portia tightly.

She took the opportunity to get out of London herself. She'd already taken two days out to visit Yorkshire, in search of the elusive Miss Maria Colding. Now she booked a flight to Geneva. She wanted to check out a painting sold thirty years ago to a wealthy Swiss, listed only as 'School of Teller'—with luck it would prove to be by Teller himself.

She mentioned her plans to Tom that evening. They shared a house in Kensington, which had been divided into two generous flats, with a guest flat in the basement. The arrangement suited them both—it gave them enough privacy, but each other's company when they wanted it.

Tom seemed to be over the flu, but he looked haggard and heavy-eyed, and definitely not firing on all cylinders. Portia frowned, feeling guilty. The last thing she wanted to do was to complain to her brother that she was being pursued by Diego Saez. Tom might feel he had to impose some kind of brotherly protection around her, and, little as she knew the world of high finance, she had nous enough to realise that for Tom to be on bad terms with a man like Diego Saez was not a good idea.

'You need a break,' she told him. 'Can't you get away

from the bank and go down to Salton for a while? It would do you good. You know you hate London.'

'I can't get away right now,' her brother answered shortly.

She looked at him. Everything about Loring Lanchester bored her stupid, but poor Tom had to deal with it, like it or not. As the son and heir, he'd had no option but to step into his father's shoes. She, a mere daughter, had been free to follow her own consuming interest—the history of art.

'Is everything all right?' she asked suddenly. 'I mean at the bank.'

Tom's grey eyes shifted away. 'Just the general economic downturn, that's all. It's hitting everyone.'

Not Diego Saez, she thought acidly. The man had just bid a record sum for a Dutch still-life at auction. It had left everyone gasping.

But she wasn't going to think about Diego Saez any more than she had to.

'Well, don't work too hard anyway,' she told her brother. 'Do you want me to invite Felicity to stay for a while? She'd cheer you up! You know, you really ought to get on with things and fix a wedding date. What on earth's keeping you?'

Tom's expression changed. 'There's no rush, you know. And anyway...' He paused, then went on, 'Maybe we're not right for each other.'

Portia stared. 'Not right? I've never seen two people more right for each other! Felicity's crazy about you—and I should know, it's me she confides in whenever I'm down at Salton.' She frowned suddenly. 'Don't tell me you've gone off her, Tom?'

He looked uncomfortable. 'I'm…very fond…of Fliss, but—well, she could probably do a lot better than marry me, you know! Rupert Bellingham would marry her like a shot!'

'Yes, but she's not in love with Rupert Bellingham—she's in love with you!'

'She'd be a lot better off marrying him,' Tom said doggedly. 'And he's got a handle!'

'Felicity doesn't want to be Lady Bellingham—she wants to be Mrs Lanchester. So I simply don't see why you don't agree a wedding date and get on with it!'

Tom looked hunted suddenly. 'For God's sake, stop nagging me!' he bit out.

She stared, both astonished and shocked. Tom never lost his temper at her, or indeed anyone. He saw her expression and looked apologetic.

'I'm sorry—it's just that—well, like I said, there's a lot on my plate at the moment at the bank.'

She was immediately sympathetic—and indignant. 'You really ought to get Uncle Martin to pull his weight more. He *is* still the chairman after all—and he makes such a *point* of it. He shouldn't leave everything to you.'

Tom made no reply, just looked tireder. Not wanting to plague him any longer, let alone about the inertia of their late father's friend and partner Martin Loring, she simply bade him goodnight and went off up to her own flat.

The trip to Geneva proved to be a waste of time. The painting was, indeed, nothing more than a work from Teller's studio.

Her mood when she returned was not good, and what she wanted to do was stay in that evening, have a long bath and an early night. But she had promised Hugh Mackerras she would go with him to a select reception to launch a new exhibition at one of the prestigious private London art galleries, and, knowing that he valued her for her social contacts, she felt obliged not to let him down.

Would Diego Saez be there that evening? she wondered. Surely to God he ought to be leaving London by now, instead of tormenting her!

But in case he hadn't, in case he was still haunting London and the art world, she dressed with particular care that evening. She did not make the mistake of wearing that over-concealing outfit again, but she did, all the same, select her attire deliberately. This time she wore a heather-coloured cocktail dress that she had realised was a mistake the moment she'd got it home. It had languished in a corner of her wardrobe ever since. The colour made her look washed out, and the cap sleeves cut her upper arm at just the wrong point.

But it made her feel safe.

Hearing her cab at the door, she set off.

The gallery was in a large, double-fronted Georgian mansion a street or so back from Piccadilly, and the rooms where the reception was being held were already crowded with familiar faces. Portia's progress towards Hugh on the far side of the room was inevitably slow as she was caught up in greeting and being greeted along the way. Her eyes rapidly scanned the space for the man she did *not* wish to see there, and to her relief she caught no sight of his tall, broad-shouldered, olive-skinned frame. She started to relax, paused to engage in some social chit-chat with a female acquaintance, smiled politely after the requisite length of time, and turned to continue on towards Hugh.

And realised that Diego Saez was standing right beside him.

Immediately, without her volition, she felt that wire tugging through her, felt that jittery, panicky feeling jump inside her. She could feel her heart-rate increasing, her lungs tightening.

Desperately she fought to regain control of her reactions, subdue them, force them down below the cool, composed surface she liked to present to the world.

It was so obvious that she'd been heading for Hugh that she could hardly change course now. As for latching on to someone else to talk to until the danger was over and Diego Saez had moved on—suddenly there was no one else within chatting distance. With a fateful feeling of helplessness, she bowed to the inevitable and continued to head towards Hugh.

Deliberately she did not look at the man with him.

But she had to fight herself to stop herself doing so. Something inside her made her *want* to look, made her want to let her eyes go to him, see those dark, heavy-lidded eyes, that strong nose, the high-cut cheekbones and that sensual mouth that so disturbed her…

Her feet reached Hugh. He greeted her in his customary fashion and then immediately said, 'Mr Saez was expressing an interest in Regency portraiture. I told him you were something of a specialist.'

She lifted her chin, realising she would have to look at Diego Saez because social convention demanded she did not cut him, as she longed to do.

Nevertheless, it took a distinct effort to keep her voice cool as she made her reply.

'Hardly. Benjamin Teller, in whom I specialise, was a very minor artist in comparison with the likes of Lawrence and Romney.'

She took refuge in prosing on, trying hard to look at a point somewhere over Diego Saez's tall shoulder.

'Is he increasing in value?'

The deep, accented tone of his voice jarred through her. So did his question. Typical of a financier, she thought acidly.

'For someone of your means, Mr Saez, Benjamin Teller is nothing more than small fry. Quite off your radar.'

She could see that her offhand reply had both taken Hugh aback and displeased him.

'Teller would be an astute investment,' he contributed smoothly. 'He's considerably under-appreciated, I believe.'

A caustic look lit Portia's eye. 'You sound like a dealer, Hugh,' she said dryly. She turned back to Diego Saez, who had singled her out to torment her with his disturbing attention. 'Dealers,' she said, with malicious lightness. 'They see art only in pound signs—or dollars or euros. As do investment buyers, of course.' She smiled pointedly. 'As worth nothing but money.'

She looked right into her tormentor's face.

A strange, measuring look entered his eye. And something more.

Dangerous—

She put the thought aside. Ridiculous! Of course Diego Saez wasn't dangerous. He was just an over-rich, sexually spoilt man who wanted to take her to bed simply because she'd made it perfectly obvious she did not want him to!

'You consider money something of little value, then, Miss Lanchester?'

The deep voice was probing.

'In comparison with art, yes,' she answered tartly.

He smiled. Deep lines indented around his mouth. She felt something tug at her internally. Then, as he spoke, she noticed that the expression in his eyes did not match the one on his face.

'But then you have never been without money, have you? Or, indeed—' there was a sardonic tone to his voice '—without art. I notice that at least two of the paintings in this exhibition are on loan from your family.'

She ignored both the tug that had come again inside her, and the tone of his voice, merely glad that the subject was still the relatively safe one of British landscape paintings. If she *had* to have a conversation with Diego Saez at least let it be about something that innocuous.

'Yes—my brother has loaned a Gainsborough and a Robert Wilson.'

'Show me.'

There was a command in his voice that put her back up automatically. But before she could reply his hand had come around her elbow, and with a brief, dismissive smile at Hugh he started to lead her away.

Her stomach clenched, and she had to force herself not to jerk away from his hold on her. As if he knew it, and it amused him, he merely continued to lead her inexorably away from Hugh.

She wanted to make a fuss, detach herself instantly, but

knew that she could not. Not here. Had it been any other man who had commandeered her like that she might have made the attempt, but something about Diego Saez told her that he would not be easily dislodged. Schooling her expression, she let him guide her away, wishing that the touch of his hand on her bare elbow was not making the tugging feeling in her insides ten times worse.

'The Wilson is through here,' she said, in a voice sounding as uninterested in what was happening to her as she could make it. She'd checked the catalogue earlier on, to see where the two paintings had been hung.

'I'd prefer to see the Gainsborough,' Diego Saez replied, and altered direction, his frame leaning very slightly into her path to make her change course. Not wanting the slightest contact with him, she moved instantly.

On top of everything else that was wracking her nerves by this wretched encounter, she was conscious of a reluctance to show him the Gainsborough. It was of Salton, and suddenly—she could not tell why—she did not want him seeing it. It was too…intrusive.

But short of making an unacceptable scene she had no option. Stiffly she walked beside him to gain the room where this section of Gainsboroughs was hanging.

'Which is yours?'

'My brother's,' corrected Portia. 'Over there on the far wall, third from the left.'

He walked towards it, dropping her elbow. She followed beside him.

He stopped a few feet from the painting and stood looking at it.

Portia gazed too, and felt a familiar emotion well through her. It was so powerful that it even, for a moment, blanked out the disturbing presence of the man beside her.

She gazed in familiar pleasure at the painting, which usually hung in their entrance hall at Salton.

Very little had changed since one of the greatest artists in the English canon had captured the likeness of Salton's honey-coloured South façade. Some of the trees framing the lake from where the view had been taken were now gone, and some were far mightier than the saplings they had been two hundred years ago and more. There were more flowerbeds now, and her great-great grandfather had planted an azalea arboretum to the east of the house a hundred years ago, but otherwise she felt she might as well step straight into the picture for all the difference the intervening centuries had made.

She felt her expression soften. Though she would never live at Salton she had grown up there, and it was as beloved to her as her brother was. As for Tom—he *was* Salton. It was his home, and the place he belonged to. He held it in trust for his son to come, and for his grandson. For future generations of Lanchesters, just as past generations had held it in trust for Tom. An uninterrupted inheritance for over four centuries.

A voice beside her spoke.

'Is it for sale?'

Her head swung round. She was totally taken aback.

'Of course not!' There was shock in her voice. 'And nor is the Wilson!' she added, before he could ask about that, too. 'This is an exhibition of paintings for public view, a temporary exhibition gathered together from museums and private collections around the world, Mr Saez—it is not a saleroom!'

'I was not referring to the paintings. I mean the house—Salton.'

The sardonic look was back in his face, but she ignored it. She was simply staring at him in total disbelief.

'Salton?'

'Yes.'

She took a deep breath. 'Mr Saez, I appreciate that not being English, or indeed European, you may not understand that country houses traditionally continue within the same family unless adverse circumstances dictate otherwise. In the mid-twentieth century, for example, there was a great selling off of country estates for that reason, and many of those now do change hands fairly regularly—I'm sure any of the country house specialist property agencies could help you if you are interested in buying an estate in this country,' she finished quellingly.

'Thank you for the information, Miss Lanchester.' The deep voice sounded even more sardonic, and she felt a flush go through her. 'However, the concept of ancestral property is not unknown in South America—nor are the sentiments that accompany that concept.'

There was a bite in his voice that she could not fail to detect.

She felt colour flare in her cheekbones. Of course a man of his background—the South American megaplutocracy—would know all about vast inherited estates! But she ignored it. 'In which case I can only be astonished that you thought to ask such an extraordinary question!'

'Extraordinary?' There was suddenly a flat note in Diego Saez's voice. 'You yourself concede that "adverse circumstances" can make selling an attractive proposition.'

She went on staring at him.

'There are no "adverse circumstances" surrounding Salton, Mr Saez,' she bit out. 'And therefore no possibility whatsoever that it will ever come on to the market! It is not for sale, nor will it be—please disabuse yourself of that idea!'

Something showed in his eyes, and was veiled. Then, with a twist of his mouth, he said 'Everything is for sale, Portia. *Everything*. Don't you know that yet?'

There was mockery in his voice now, an open taunt. And more—derision.

She felt for a moment as if something had crawled over her flesh.

Then, recovering, she lifted her chin.

'In your world, perhaps, Mr Saez. But not in mine!'

There was something strange in his eyes.

'Do you think not?' He paused. 'Are you really the innocent you look?' The expression in his eyes changed, and suddenly Portia felt that hot wire drawing through her again. 'You look so extraordinarily *untouched*—and yet I'm told you were engaged for nearly two years.'

His hand reached out, the backs of his fingers drawing down the side of her throat, her jaw. She could not breathe. Could only feel the hammering of her heart. She wanted to move, but she could not—*could not.*

CHAPTER FOUR

WITHOUT her realising, without her even being aware of it, he had moved in on her. His body was closer to hers now, shielding her from the doorway on the far side of the room that led back to the reception. There was no one else here, it was just the two of them. She could inhale the scent of him, that mix of masculinity and expensive, exclusive aftershave. She could feel the heat of his body—and the heat of her own, as her skin flushed.

'Don't—' Her voice came on a faint breath. The panicky, jittery feeling was shivering through her, her breath was shallow.

'Don't? Is that what you told your fiancé?'

There was mockery as well as questioning in his voice. And taunting too—she could hear that loud and clear.

She could feel his breath fanning her face, hear the husk in his voice. 'They tell me you're cold, Portia, as cold as the snow. But you're not—I can feel it—here...'

His fingers pressed lightly, oh, so lightly, against the pulse in her throat. It leapt at his touch, flushing blood through her already heated veins. She was gazing up at him, eyes dilating.

Watching, breathless, helpless, as his mouth descended.

'I can feel it here,' he murmured, and his mouth took hers.

It moved with slow, leisurely movement across her lips, as his fingers splayed out across her throat, imprisoning her.

Blood drummed through her, blood and faintness and a sensation so blissful she wanted it to go on and on, as his mouth moved on hers.

It was a different world, another universe. Never, ever,

had any man kissed her like this. She didn't like being kissed much—even by those few men she had liked enough to let them do what they had so evidently wanted to do, even though she'd wished they hadn't, had wished they'd been content, as she had been, with a comfortable brush of the lips—swift and soon over and done with.

This kiss was neither.

It was cool—with possession, with casual tasting, with an assumption of intimacy, of pleasure, that dissolved the very bones in her body.

He let her go, lifting his mouth from hers, slipping his fingers from her skin, and she stood there, swaying, blinded, dazed.

'Fools,' he mocked. 'To call you cold…' He touched along her parted lips with the tips of his fingers. 'At my touch, for me, you are not cold…'

He dropped his hands away from her face to her bare upper arms and put her away from him. She would have stumbled but for his hold, steadying her. He stood looking down at her a moment, his hands still around her arms, surveying her.

His eyes lit with amusement—and more—as he looked at her unflattering attire.

'Did you really think that you could disguise your beauty in a dress like that?' His voice dropped, 'Do you think that you can run from me? It's time,' he said softly, and something in his voice sent shivers down her spine. 'Time to stop running, Portia. It has been amusing, but…' His voice changed again, becoming nothing more than its familiar accented timbre. 'Now...' His left hand slipped down to cup her elbow and he let go of her other arm, steering her from the room. 'We had better return to the reception or our absence will draw comments.'

The heat in her skin flared, and she realised suddenly, horribly, just what had happened. Diego Saez had kissed her. A man who represented *everything* that she hated most—the kind of man who treated a woman like a conquest and herself as his quarry. Stomach churning, she stalked at his side, back into the crowded reception. Her breath was coming and going sharply in her throat and she had to fight down her emotions, slam the lid of social conduct down tightly upon them—and make her escape as soon as she could do so.

Emotions chewed through her. Outrage at what he had just done so supremely casually, helping himself to her as if she were a fresh, ripe peach on a market stall! But worse, far worse that the stinging outrage, was the melting, dissolving weakness that was still echoing through her body, a physical memory of what she had just experienced.

Then, overlaying both, a new emotion thrust up into her. Blind panic.

A sense of danger pressed down upon her, so intense it was almost frightening.

But she could not get away. As if sensing her feelings, Diego Saez merely strengthened his hold on her elbow, walking her through the reception, pausing as he went to exchange social chit-chat with others as they passed.

And as they made their uneven progress Portia, through the emotions panicking her, became aware of yet something else.

People were looking at her. She could see it in their eyes—speculation, some covert, some blatant, over her presence at Diego Saez's side.

And she realised with a horrible, hollowing sense of horror that finally he was making his move on her. He was not going to let her evade him any longer.

She heard his words in her head, terrifying her.

Time to stop running…

But she *had* to run—had to get him to leave her alone! To accept that however many other women were stupid enough to fall into his bed for a month or two, she would not be among them!

However much he calmly intended to have her.

Diego Saez, hand still at her elbow, holding her at his

side, was proclaiming to all the world that she was the woman he wanted—and was sublimely confident of getting.

Feeling as if she were some kind of conquered slave, trailing along with the triumphant Roman general, she could do nothing except let herself be steered through the room. Her lips were smiling, as if in a rictus, her voice was murmuring the required niceties, and all the time she was feeling the heat flushing through her like a ghastly wave machine, over and over and over again.

Heat and memory—memory of that kiss…

He did not move from her side—nor let her leave. As if in some kind of nightmare she had to talk, and smile, and endure the worst ordeal of all—the knowing looks, the pointed remarks, that Diego Saez's constant presence at her side inevitably drew. She ignored them doggedly, desperately, calling on all her reserves of self-control to get her through to the end.

But was it going to end? After what seemed a perpetual eternity it came to her, with a new wave of horror, that they were progressing slowly but surely towards the exit. And then, through the blankness in her head, she heard that deep, accented voice saying to whoever he was speaking to at the time, 'Another evening, perhaps. Tonight I have a prior engagement.'

He glanced down at her, and whoever it was gave a knowing laugh and moved away. And then one of the gallery staff was there, proffering her jacket, and the man at her side was slipping it on her, his hands drawing it up over her shoulders. Her face and her body were as stiff as board as, making smooth, bland farewells, Diego ushered her out on to the pavement.

She was like a zombie, without will or volition of her own. Diego Saez had taken her over.

Her heart slugged in her chest, panic prickling all through her body, as she climbed into the waiting car, where a chauffeur was holding open the door, and Diego Saez folded his long, lean body in after her.

This can't be happening, she thought. *It can't!*

She sat ramrod-straight in her seat, staring doggedly in front of her through the dividing glass at the back of the chauffeur's head as he took his place, pulling the limo out into the street.

She wanted to scream, to shout, to leap from the car. But she could do none of those things. Something had taken control of her—something more powerful than she had ever felt in her life before.

Of their own volition—certainly not with her conscious will—she felt her head turn, her eyes rest on the tall, dark figure sitting beside her in the far corner of the wide rear seat of the limo. His long legs were stretched out.

He smiled. A slow, sensual smile.

'Well, Portia—here we are. Alone at last.'

His mocking tone sent shivers through her.

From somewhere deep inside she found the strength to speak.

'I would be much obliged, Mr Saez, if you would please drop me off at the next taxi rank or Underground station. I have no intention of spending any further time with you.'

She wanted her voice to sound arctic—but it merely trembled.

His presence overpowered her. It was like a physical weight—touching her, crushing the breath from her lungs.

'We're going to dinner,' he replied, his casual indifference to her rigidly civil request galling her. 'I've reserved a table at Claridge's.'

Her eyes flashed in disbelief at what he had just said. Outrage soared up over the panicky feeling that was flushing through her.

'Then you may *un*-reserve it, Mr Saez. I am not dining with you!'

Looking him in the eye had been a mistake. As she met that heavy-lidded gaze, resting on her, a feeling of hot, molten lava started to flow viscously through her veins.

Confusion churned in her.

What's happening to me? Why is he doing this? How is he doing this? I don't want him, I don't like him, I want to get out of the car and run, and run and run…

Danger pressed all around her. It was tangible—a dark, disturbing presence.

And more than danger.

Something she would not give a name to. Something that had leapt in her throat as she let his dark, dissolving gaze hold her.

He reached a hand out to her. Lightly—casually—devastatingly—he drew the backs of his fingers along her cheek.

She jerked away as if a thousand volts had just gone through her.

'Don't touch me!'

There was panic in her voice.

Long lashes swept down over his eyes.

'But you want me to touch you, Portia. And I want to touch you. Very much…'

He leant towards her. She could do nothing. Not even shrink back into the corner of her seat.

Her eyes fluttered shut.

His mouth moved on hers, long fingers tilting up her face to his. That slow, dissolving lava was molten in her veins, her body.

She tried to summon outrage, tried to want to push him away, shout at him—slap his face!

But she could not. She could only sit there, her body dissolving, at his touch.

I don't let men do this. But Diego Saez, who only wanted to amuse himself with her for a bare handful of weeks, she let him. Let him help himself—shamingly, humiliatingly, *totally*, to her mouth…

He pulled away and dimly, very dimly, she became aware that the car had stopped.

He drew a finger across her swollen lips. Her body was trembling. His eyes were dark, so dark.

'Tonight, Portia, it begins.'

He smiled at her. A long, sensual smile.

Absolutely confident.

Supremely expectant.

It was the smile that did it. Broke through the dissolving, weakening paralysis that was holding her in a helpless thrall. As if surfacing from a deep, drowning wave, she felt a new emotion surge through her. Virulent. Overpowering.

She was icy with rage.

Rage at Diego Saez for daring, *daring* to do that to her. For helping himself to her as if he had every right to do so, as if all he had to do was simply reach out and *sample* her…

And she had let him. Had let him do exactly that. Had offered no resistance—none—as he had made free with her as no man had ever done. And for a man like Diego Saez to do that to her—arrogant and spoilt by legions of women drooling over him, a hedonistic sensualist for whom women were an appetite, an indulgence. Everything, *everything* she despised in a man.

Good God, if she hadn't liked Geoffrey kissing her, touching her—a man she'd respected, liked…loved…how could she bear to have someone like Diego Saez kiss her…touch her…?

But she *had* let him kiss her. Touch her. Had let him walk off with her in front of everyone, signalling to the whole world what his intentions to her were. Portia Lanchester—ice-cold Portia Lanchester—was about to feel the heat…

About to be Diego Saez's next amusement.

The icy rage shot through her again. But this time it had a different target.

Herself.

Fear shivered through her. Somewhere deep inside, in a part of her she had never known existed but which, now she did, terrified her, she knew that Diego Saez could exert a power over her that she had never imagined.

With every ounce of her being she fought it. Rejected it.

Shame flooded through her. That of all the men in the world it should be a man like Diego Saez who could reduce her to such a condition.

She felt the rage against herself, her own weakness, her own folly, as ice in her veins. She clung to it. It was her saviour, her one chance of escaping with her skin whole. Because if she stayed…

She flung open the door of the car and climbed out. The chauffeur was still getting out of the driver's seat, but she didn't wait. She stood on the pavement, rigid with lashing fury. She had to keep angry—she *had* to!

Diego Saez got out and said something to the chauffeur. He nodded and got back into the limo. It began to pull away from the kerb.

'Come,' said the man at her side, and slid his hand under her elbow.

She jerked away violently. She was trembling with emotion that this arrogant man was simply assuming that she would fall into his bed like a ripe peach, just because he wanted her to.

'Take your hand off me!' Her voice was loaded with anger as she stepped back.

The rest of the world had disappeared. Somewhere in her mind she realised she was standing in Brook Street, outside Claridge's. There was a doorman not three feet away, and several other people disgorging from a taxi.

She had to get away.

Urgency overwhelmed her, overriding everything else. She started to walk away, heading past the hotel façade towards the traffic lights on the corner. Her heels clicked on the damp pavement. Her breathing was short. Heart pounding in a horrible, sick fashion. There was pressure inside her head.

She started to walk faster.

There were footsteps behind her. Rapid, heavy.

A hand clamped around her shoulder, halting her. Turning her around.

'Portia—'

His voice sounded impatient. There was a dark look in his eye. His prey was escaping, walking out on him. Diego Saez's prey for the night was daring to walk out on him…

Something, it might have been hysteria, started to climb in her throat. She crushed it down.

'Leave me alone!' she snapped at him, trying to jerk herself loose.

But this time it did not work. His fingers bit into her.

Panic stabbed at her. He wasn't letting her go. He was holding on to her. Touching her…

'How dare you manhandle me?' The words cut from her, clipped and furious. 'How dare you touch me? You *disgust* me!' A sharp, searing breath sliced through her throat and her chin flew up. He was standing there so tall, overpoweringly so. He seemed to loom over her. His face, as she threw her angry words at him, darkened. She didn't care. Didn't care that she was making a scene right outside Claridge's. Didn't care that she was finally venting that terrifying surge of emotion he aroused in her.

She stepped back. 'Did you think—did you really think—' her voice was icy with scorn '—that you could just *help yourself* to me?' Her eyes were cold grey pinpricks, flashing disdain, disgust. Outrage. 'Do you really think that I would even *consider* having an affair with *you*? Of *all* people? A man with *your* history? *Your* reputation? *Your* past? Do you really think I would *demean* myself with a man like *you*? Do you think your *money* makes you acceptable?'

Something changed in his eyes. Something that just for a second sent a shaft of fear through her. And then, like a metal gate slicing down, it was gone. His face was like a mask. Completely expressionless.

Her breath was coming in sharp, painful jags, like ice in

her lungs. Her chin had flown up, her hands clutching her open jacket across her, her shoulders rigid, eyes arctic with rejection.

He was standing quite still, she realised. Completely motionless. But it was the stillness of a jaguar poised in a jungle clearing, every muscle under complete, absolute control.

The still before the kill.

Fear stabbed through her again, countering the icy rage that still consumed her, which itself was forcing down yet another emotion—one that she could not cope with, could not admit or acknowledge or allow.

With one part of her mind she knew she had behaved disgracefully, lowering herself to speak in such a way to him—but she had had no choice. None. She *had* to protect herself from him—any way she could.

He was just so, so dangerous…he made her feel out of control.

He spoke. His voice was without emotion.

'In which case, if those are your sentiments, I will bid you goodnight.'

He turned on his heel and walked into the hotel. His pace was neither hurried nor slow.

He was gone.

Alone on the pavement in the chill spring night, Portia stood, face frozen, everything frozen.

Slowly, jerkily, she started to walk.

Diego Saez strode down the black and white squared hallway, away from the hotel lobby towards the bar. He walked in and up to the bar. The barman took one look at him and was there instantly.

'Whisky.'

There was a nerve working in his cheek.

A single malt was soon in front of him and he lifted the glass and knocked it back in one.

An image burned in his head.

Not of Portia Lanchester.

Another woman.

Chic, immaculately dressed, with inky blue hair coiled like a snake at the back of her head. Her lips were very red.

Her eyes were black, as black as sin. Nothing like the cool, cutting grey of Portia Lanchester.

But the expression in them was the same.

Disdain. Revulsion. Horror.

He heard the voice in his head again.

'*You?* The son of Carmita? It isn't possible!'

A stream of Spanish had followed. Foul, insulting, vicious. Her heavily beringed hand, flashing with diamonds and emeralds, had flown up, pointing dramatically to the door.

'Get out! Get out or I'll have you thrown out!'

Above everything from that scene, everything he remembered in coruscating detail, it was that—the absolute disbelief in Mercedes de Carvello's voice. She had been completely, totally unable to believe that the son of her maid had returned—through her own front door, walking into her drawing room—and told her that he now owned the *estancia*.

It had been the sweetest moment of his life.

And the most bitter.

For it had come too late for the two people for whom he had bought the *estancia*. His father—dead for fifteen years of a cancer caused by the carcinogenic agents knowingly used on the *estancia*'s banana plantations—and his mother, fatally knocked down on the *estancia* drive by Mercedes herself in her sports car, which she'd been driving at eighty miles an hour with a bottle of champagne inside her.

And that bitterness had made him stand there while Mercedes de Carvello, who had treated each and every one of the myriad staff who'd served her like the dirt she'd thought them, had tried to throw him from the house he had once never even been allowed to enter. But now, thanks to his own punishingly hard escape from the poverty he'd been born to, and thanks to the stupid, reckless extravagance of her dead husband Esteban de Carvello, he owned it—every last inch of it—and the vast estate that went with it.

His to do with as he liked. Whatever he liked.

A place Mercedes de Carvello no longer had any right to be.

Just as she had once told a twelve-year-old boy, his mown-down mother hardly cold in her grave, that he had no right to be there any more. She had thrown him off the estate, banning all the other workers from helping him. For he had dared, *dared* to call her a murderess to her face for killing his mother.

He had left, taking nothing with him—for he possessed nothing, she had told him—and had walked the long, weary miles, day after day, week after week, to the city, his feet bleeding, the flesh hanging from his bones, starving like so many other unwanted, surplus, valueless boys in his home country.

Taking with him nothing but the burning, punishing desire for justice.

A justice he had meted out those long, long years later, when he had ordered Mercedes de Carvello from the home she no longer possessed.

Slowly, very slowly, his eyes refocused. Came back to the present.

And saw another face—another image. Cool, blonde, English.

Filled with revulsion.

Disdain.

For him.

The barman had come back to his end of the bar. Diego pushed his empty whisky glass towards him.

'Another one,' he said.

His eyes were dark and shuttered. His face expressionless.

Silently the barman refilled his whisky glass.

CHAPTER FIVE

PORTIA stood by the sash window in the Morning Room, gazing out over the lawns. Splashed across the green, all the way down to the lake, daffodils nodded and danced in the breeze. Cloudlets scudded across the bright spring sky.

She gave a sigh of contentment. The Morning Room was one of her favourites at Salton—its delicate rosewood furniture with a slight sense of chinoiserie, the trellised, hand-blocked wallpaper, and, of course, the wonderful view down to the lake.

Slowly, as she stood gazing out over the sea of gold and green, a sense of peace, of safety, started to soothe along the edges of her torn, ragged nerves.

Here at Salton she would be safe.

She had driven down the very next day, leaving nothing but a terse phone message for Hugh to say she was catching up on some unused leave. Then she had set off, reaching Salton before lunch.

She had driven as if a devil were in pursuit.

And he is a devil, she thought. *Taunting me. Tempting me.*

She had not slept—had been tormented by dreams. Hot, disturbing dreams, where Diego Saez hunted her down a maze of corridors, pursuing her steadily, remorselessly, until he had her trapped…

Then he advanced on her. Pulled her into his arms.

Even now, standing here, gazing out over the timeless, peaceful view of the gardens, if she let her guard down for a moment, an instant, the memories were there, leaping into her mind, clutching at her.

I don't want him. I don't…

She repeated the mantra to herself, clinging to it.

It was insane that she should want Diego Saez. Insane to want a man like that.

She felt her breasts prickling beneath the cashmere of her sweater and turned away sharply.

No, she would *not* let herself be taken over like this. It was like an illness, that was all. A bug in her system. For some ludicrous, absurd, ridiculous reason Diego Saez, with his heavy-lidded eyes and his sensual mouth, had got past her defences. Defences she had erected painstakingly, doggedly, ever since she had realised so devastatingly that for her sex was a disaster—it left her cold. Untouchable.

In her mind, she heard Susie saying impatiently, 'Oh, for heaven's sake, Portia, Geoffrey was just wrong for you, that's all! That's why you didn't like sex with him. And *that's* why you need someone like Diego Saez! There isn't a woman alive who wouldn't enjoy sex with a man like him!'

For a hot and shameful instant she saw a vision of herself in a bedroom, with Diego Saez advancing on her. His hands were unknotting his tie, shrugging off his jacket. His eyes were focused on her, dark and knowing. And with one intention only…

She suddenly felt the sensual quickening of her own body. Then, like a lid slamming down, she regained control.

She would go for a walk. Out in the grounds. Round the lake. Pick some daffodils. Arrange some flowers in the afternoon. Have tea in the library.

Feel safe.

Be safe.

Resolutely, she walked out of the room.

The long, blowy walk did her good. She always went for a good long walk when she came down to Salton, whatever the weather or the time of year. It was a ritual, so that she could find the peace she knew she would always find here.

Even now.

She had not put Diego Saez out of her mind completely.

That was impossible. What he had done to her was so devastating, so frightening, that it would take a long, long time to get over it. He had broken through her defences and destroyed her peace of mind. How he had done it she still did not know.

And that made it even more frightening.

But here at Salton she was safe. Here she would find her peace of mind again. Here she would find the balm that she needed. Her safe, familiar world.

And so very precious to her.

Even more so to Tom.

But then Salton *was* the Lanchester family. Had been for generations and generations. She could not even begin to imagine not being part of Salton—Salton not being part of her, part of her family. It was a sentiment, she knew, that those who did not have the privilege—and it was a privilege, she was supremely conscious of that—of being so inextricably linked with a house, a place, found it difficult to understand. It was not a question of wealth—a Welsh hill farmer struggling desperately to survive against the hardships of the modern agricultural economy would feel just as passionate about the land he farmed, the land he owned. That sense of kinship, devotion, to a particular piece of the earth, for which no other place, however beautiful, could substitute, a kinship earned through time, hundreds of years, was something that was hard to understand if it had not been experienced.

She experienced it again now, as she experienced it every time, as she tramped in gum boots down across the lawns, around the lake, through the woods and across several fields to come back up to the house by way of the azalea arboretum. She made a swathe through the sea of daffodils again, gathering them up in a bountiful armful and going on to add sufficient greenery from the shrubbery plantings around the edge of the lawn.

By the time she came back indoors she was pleasantly tired—and spiritually refreshed. Her instinct to fly to Salton had been the right one. Here, she knew, she would find the peace of mind that had been ripped from her.

Here she would forget that face with the heavy-lidded, darkly knowing eyes, and the mocking, sensual mouth.

Here, Diego Saez could not endanger her.

She laid down her bounty of daffodils and greenery on the cool marble surface beside the old stone sink, and spent a happy hour arranging flowers in the flower room. It was a soothing occupation, and the sweet, fresh scent of the daffodils was familiar, her fingers working so deftly, that the time flew by.

It flew by for the next three days. Three days in which she succumbed to the peaceful, familiar, uneventful rhythm of life at Salton. She did not go out, did not even phone round her acquaintances to let them know she was there. She didn't want to socialise. All she wanted to do was stay safe at Salton.

She was not bored. She was never bored at Salton. Although Tom had a professional estate manager to look after the farms, the house and grounds were under his direct remit. And until he married she was, in effect, mistress of the house. While they were in London the Tillets, the couple who kept Salton running on oiled wheels, either phoned or faxed to stay in touch as necessary, but the moment she or Tom appeared in person they were always pounced on.

Now Mrs Tillet, the housekeeper, had a hundred things to check with her, that had cropped up since her last visit, from a spot of damp noticed in one of the upper bedrooms, to whether or not the sun-faded curtains in the music room needed to be relined yet. Outdoors, Fred Hermitage, the head gardener, needed decisions on a hundred more items on his list, from repainting the interior of the orangery to replanting the herbaceous border below the west terrace. And within the community there were regular matters to attend to.

With the summer coming, the list of Salton's regular open days needed to be decided, and that required her to liaise with the vicar's wife as to what the parish committee would prefer and which charities they would like proceeds to go to. The local cub pack had requested permission to hold their annual treasure trail in the woods that formed part of the demesne lands, the headmistress of the village junior school wanted the ten-year-olds to tour the house as part of their history curriculum, and the amateur dramatic group wanted to stage *A Midsummer Night's Dream* beside the Greek temple folly on the far side of the lake.

It was all safe, familiar, reassuring—a million miles away from Diego Saez and his powerful, disturbing presence.

Here at Salton she was safe from it. From him. He could not intrude, could not threaten her fragile peace of mind.

She was just heading upstairs to change, on the third afternoon after her arrival, when Mrs Tillet hurried out into the hall. Portia paused on the stair. She had come indoors after a vigorous session digging up the herbaceous border with Fred Hermitage, emptying wheelbarrows of discarded vegetation and mulching in fertiliser and humus, and her ancient, baggy corduroy trousers needed a good wash. So did she.

But her mood was good. She loved gardening, even when it left her with an aching back and tired muscles.

'Hello, Mrs T. What's up?' she asked with a smile.

'Your brother has just phoned, Miss Portia,' the housekeeper told her. 'He said to tell you that he'll be coming down tomorrow.'

Portia's smile widened. 'Oh, I'm so glad, Mrs T! Tom's been overworking horribly, and I've been telling him to take a break from that wretched bank and come down here for a while! He can relax and recharge before going back to town again!'

'He did say, Miss Portia, that he would be bringing a business acquaintance with him,' answered Mrs Tillet.

Portia's smile turned to a grimace. 'Oh, how wretched! I suppose he's going to stay the night. Is the Blue Room made up? He can go in there. Or is it a couple? Did Tom say? If so, then the Oak Room would be better.'

'A single gentleman, so I understand,' elaborated Mrs Tillet.

'The Blue Room it is, then, Mrs T. Do you want a hand getting it ready?'

The housekeeper shook her head. 'I've got Betty Wilkins and Marjorie Sanders coming up this afternoon and all day tomorrow. We'll see to everything. Would you care to choose the menu for tomorrow night?'

Portia shook her head. 'You can do menus blindfolded, Mrs T. I'll stick to the flowers—I'll have to go and raid the glasshouses and risk wrecking Fred's wrath upon me for taking his prime specimens!'

Later, as she sat curled up on the leather sofa in the library, in front of a crackling wood fire, she wondered who Tom was bringing down. Salton was often used for business entertaining, and Portia was no stranger to acting as hostess when she was here. She wondered whether she should phone Felicity, suggest she come over as well, to make it four for dinner, but decided it might be a bit too pushy on her part. She had not forgotten Tom snapping at her when she'd gone on at him to propose to the girl he was so obviously in love with.

She frowned. Was it just overwork that was making him so short-tempered? Or a persistent bug that made him look so haggard all the time? Or were things tricky at the bank? Trickier, that was, than they normally were, with Uncle Martin wanting to have all the privileges of his position and do none of the work.

Words uttered in a deep, accented drawl echoed in her memory. *Adverse circumstances.* She pressed her mouth tightly. Diego Saez was being absurd. There were no 'adverse circumstances' surrounding Salton. Salton had belonged to the Lanchesters for hundreds of years, through thick and thin. The bank, Loring Lanchester, provided a hefty boost to the family wealth, but Tom was not dependent on it. If necessary Salton could be self-sufficient—there were the farms, and, like so many other stately home owners, he could always go into the heritage business. Besides, both she and her brother had investment portfolios which yielded generous private incomes.

So why, deep in her bones, did she feel a frisson of fear go through her, and that dark, deep voice echo again in her head, laconically enquiring whether Salton was for sale?

More words echoed in her mind.

Everything is for sale, Portia.

A scornful look lit her eye. Yes, in Diego Saez's world everything had a price! A man as rich as he was, with a spoilt, pampered background as he had—a prince of the pampas, or whatever part of South America he came from!—*would* think like that, she thought condemningly.

Into her mind's eye came the image of his face—those hooded, knowing eyes, that cynical, sensual twist of his mouth.

That mouth, moving on hers…

Out of nowhere, like a wolf at her throat, memory gripped her. So vivid it could be happening now, again. Diego Saez helping himself to her mouth.

Shudderingly she pushed the memory away. She would not remember. She must not!

Diego Saez was gone from her life. She had got rid of him. Disposed of him. Made it very, very clear to him that his attentions were repugnant to her, his generous invitation to add her to his charming collection of temporary bed-warmers unwelcome.

She did not want Diego Saez.

And she had told him so. Spelt it out to him loud and clear, voicing all her contempt, her revulsion, for the life he lived.

He had got the message, all right. Walked away from her. Taken his dismissal and walked off.

A shiver went through her.

I got off lightly…

The words formed in her brain, and even as they formed she felt a shimmer of unease go through her.

Did men like Diego Saez walk away from what they wanted?

Tight-jawed, she reached forward for the teapot. Well, this time he would just have to accept defeat.

Portia slid the black jersey silk dress over her head, and smoothed it down over her body. It was a particular favourite for dinner parties here, whether large or small, social or business. Its graceful boat neck flattered her shoulders, and the elbow-length sleeves made her forearms slender and graceful, as did the on-the-knee hemline She slipped her feet into a pair of modest high heels, clipped a necklace around her throat, put on matching drop earrings, strapped her evening watch around her wrist, then applied her lipstick, checked her hair was still immaculate in its chignon, and headed downstairs.

Tom and his business guest would be here any moment. Even though it was unnecessary she did a quick walk around the twelve-foot mahogany table, glittering with crystal and silver, and with one of her floral arrangements centred on its length, flanked by silver candelabra. In the grate a wood fire added to the background warmth of the central heating, and on the walls an array of family portraits, landscapes and still-lifes complemented the long dark blue velvet curtains, the blue and gold patterned carpet and the mahogany sideboards and console tables. The scent of beeswax polish mingled with the freshness of the flowers and the fragrance of the burning wood.

It was a familiar and beloved scene, and Portia found herself wondering, with a smile, just how many dinner parties this room must have seen in its time, presided over by whoever was head of the house at the time.

And how many more it still would see.

She moved on to check the drawing room where, as in the dining room, everything was in perfect order. She paused in front of the fireplace, shielded from the blaze by a firescreen, and gazed at her own reflection momentarily in the glass over the mantel.

Why had Diego Saez pursued her the way he had?

Surely he could see from looking at her that she was not the type to indulge in the kind of sordid little affairs he clearly specialised in? Nor was she *his* type either—from all the photos in the celebrity magazines that Susie had insisted on showing her it seemed Diego Saez went for the sultry type. She gazed at herself a moment longer, taking in the cool, classic features that looked back at her out of clear grey eyes. She was a million miles away from the spectacular, flashy females he obviously had a taste for!

So what on earth did he see in her?

Certainly Geoffrey Chandler, she thought with a sudden pang, hadn't found it hard to find another woman to marry him, and his chosen bride was a very pretty brunette.

She turned away. She must not think about Geoffrey. It had all been such a mess. Such a horrible, painful mess. She'd hurt and humiliated him, and though it had superficially been a very civilised parting of the ways, the wound had gone deeper than she wanted to admit.

A thought drifted across her mind. Was Susie right? Did she need some kind of drastic 'cure' for her messy broken engagement? Such as a passionate, physical affair with someone like Diego Saez?

No! She wouldn't even *start* to think like that! The man's attitude to her—to sex—appalled her. Disgusted her. Treating it as if it were nothing but an appetite—to be sated on any female he decided to select, as if he were choosing from a wine list.

Her lips pressed together and she turned away from the looking glass.

As she did so she realised she was hearing the sound of a car coming along the long drive from the road, a good mile and a half away. Tom and his business guest were obviously about to arrive.

She performed one last rapid scan around the room, and waited while the car pulled up in front of the house on the gravelled forecourt. The engine cut, there was a sound of car doors slamming, feet crunching on gravel, then voices out in the hall, indistinct and muffled—Mr T taking coats, Portia assumed, as she stood, poised in front of the fire, ready for her brother and his guest. Then footsteps approached the drawing room. The double doors were opened, and in walked Tom.

Her eyes took him in, but only for the barest handful of seconds. Darkness seemed to be swirling around her. Her eyes were dragged over Tom's shoulders to the man who had walked in behind him. She felt the blood drum in her ears, her chest tighten.

It couldn't be. It just *couldn't be…*

From far away she heard Tom's voice, but it came dim, inaudible. The only sense that seemed to be operating was her vision.

And all she could see, like some horrible dream, was a tall, dark, dangerous figure that she had hoped, prayed, never to have to set eyes on again.

He was walking towards her. That same lithe, purposeful gait. The same dark, heavy-lidded eyes and strong, arresting features. His expression was shuttered, unreadable. He stopped in front of her, holding out her hand.

'Portia—' said Diego Saez, and took her nerveless hand in his.

It was like something out of a bad dream. A very bad dream. A nightmare.

It couldn't be true, it just couldn't! Diego Saez could not be standing here, in the drawing room at Salton, right in front of her.

She wanted to snatch her hand away. Was desperate to do so. But the fingers holding hers were like steel pincers. As if he knew her intention, her desire, her overwhelming instinct to pull away from him. His hand was hard, his grip unshakeable.

Then, abruptly, he let her go.

She was fighting for air. It was thick in her lungs, unbreathable. She could hear Tom speaking and with sheer force of will she turned her head towards him.

'Have you two met already? You didn't say, Señor Saez.'

There was polite surprise in his voice, and Portia was incapable of answering. Incapable of doing anything other than try and get breath into her lungs, stay upright in front of the hearth.

'Several times,' Diego Saez replied, his voice deep and accented. Portia felt the slightest shiver go through her, as though she were cold. Yet she could feel the heat from the fire diffusing through the fireguard on to the back of her stockinged legs.

'I've been buying art,' he continued, as if that was by way of an explanation.

'Ah.' Tom nodded. 'Of course.'

'In fact,' Diego Saez went on, in that same smooth, deep voice that was sending chill shivers along Portia's rigid spine, 'only last week I chanced to be at the opening of an exhibition on British eighteenth-century landscapes. The Gainsborough of Salton was very...' he paused minutely '...memorable.'

His eyes rested expressionlessly on Portia, and she knew it was not the Gainsborough he was referring to as memorable. Memory of his kiss bleached through her. She looked away.

Shock was still ricocheting inside her.

What was he *doing* here? She cast her mind about desperately. Surely Tom could not have invited him here deliberately?

Reason came to her rescue. Why shouldn't Tom have invited him? They moved in the same world of high finance, even if Diego Saez operated on a vast global scale. Desperately she found herself hoping that Tom would not have business dealings with the man! Let alone discuss them here, at Salton. At the same time she knew, with a ghastly hollow feeling that was opening up inside her, that the very last thing she could do was tell Tom just why she objected so much. How could she possibly tell her brother that, actually, Diego Saez was not welcome at Salton on account of the fact that he was trying to get her into his bed and she'd had to make her objections to his ambitions very, very plain indeed?

Of course she couldn't tell Tom. She couldn't do anything—anything at all except accept, with a trapped feeling of horrible inevitability, that she would have to spend the evening playing the gracious hostess to a man she wished to perdition! For some hideous reason Tom had seen fit to invite Diego Saez here, to Salton, on some kind of banking matter, and there was nothing, *nothing* she could do about it.

It took every ounce of her poise and self-control to get through dinner with some semblance of normality.

Throughout the long, excruciating meal—at which she did nothing more than pick—she took as little part in the conversation as she could get away with. Unfortunately, though she longed for her brother and his unwelcome guest to immerse themselves in banking talk, so she would not be required to join in, Tom insisted on making general conversation. She tried to support him out of loyalty, and also, as she belatedly realised, because he was clearly under visible stress himself. His face was still haggard, and to her own sense of anger at Diego Saez's presence at Salton was added yet more indignation that he should have accepted an invitation from a man who was so clearly unwell.

Tom was manfully trying to get through the evening, lurching from one innocuous topic to another, with Portia doing her best to behave as though the man sitting between them were nothing more than a business acquaintance. Yet all through the meal the undercurrents swirled at her feet.

She could feel the pressure of Diego Saez's presence as if it were a tangible force, was supremely aware of him seated only a few feet away from her. Desperately she tried not to watch the way his long, tanned fingers curved around the stem of his wine glass, or the silver fork he was using. Tried not to look at the lean strength of his wrist, banded with a slim gold watch, at how white the gleaming cuff looked against his skin.

But at least, she realised, he was not looking at her the way he usually did. When he spoke to her his eyes rested on her with a shuttered expression. It took her a while to realise she was finding that even more oppressive than the usual sensual assessment he subjected her to.

Her nerves started to stretch unbearably, and she longed for the meal to be over, so she could finally escape and leave them to their business discussion over the port.

She headed straight upstairs. Urgency drove her. She had thought herself safe at Salton, but Diego Saez had walked in as if he had the keys to the place!

Why? The question circled in her brain, as it had all evening, but now she could give free rein to it. He was not here because of Tom—he was here because of her. She knew it with every fibre of her being.

And she knew why.

He was angry. Angry with her for having dared to reject him. She had dared to heap scorn on him for his arrogant assumption that she was his for the taking, dared to be revulsed at his libertine lifestyle.

Well, so what? Anger lashed through her. She had spoken nothing but the truth—why should she care that he was angry at it?

Because he's dangerous…

The voice in her head stopped her restless pacing around her bedroom.

She stared, blank-eyed, ahead of her. A deep foreboding filled her. Diego Saez was here for a purpose.

Surely to God he did not think he could still succeed

with her? Did he think he could pay some midnight visit to her under her brother's own roof?

And if he does, what will you do? If, in the middle of the night, you hear the bedroom door open?

The sly, insidious question slipped past her defences. Even as it formed she stilled totally.

And into her mind came an image—heavy, sensual—of Diego Saez walking into her bedroom, taking off his tie as he advanced upon her, shrugging off his jacket, his hands going to his belt…

And her, lying back on the sheets, waiting for him…

She felt a slow, viscous heaviness subsume her body, flow through her dilating veins. Felt a flush of low, building heat mount through her, licking like a slow, sensuous flame.

Then, as if she were deep underwater, she fought her way back up to the surface. To sanity. To reality.

The reality of standing in the middle of her deserted bedroom, trying to fight down the dark, oppressive feeling of foreboding that shimmered all about her.

She slept fitfully, waking often from heavy, unremembered dreams which left a heavy feeling of dread in her heart—and something other than dread, something she would not give a name to. The knowledge that in the other wing of the house was Diego Saez, beneath the very roof of Salton, filled her with disturbing emotion. Although her room had no lock, she had placed her dressing table stool in front of the door—a frail barrier against a man such as the one who had pursued her.

But there was no nocturnal visitation, and when, finally, she fell into a proper sleep it was as dawn set the birds into their early chorus. She did not wake until gone ten. As she realised the lateness of the hour a sense of relief went through her. She had missed the ordeal of breakfasting with her brother and his unwelcome guest. With any luck he might even have left by now.

But when, after she had gone cautiously downstairs, she

enquired of Mrs Tillet, it was to learn that her brother and his guest were incarcerated in the library. Well, at least she could have her breakfast in peace, and count the time until Diego Saez took himself off.

She helped herself to tea and toast in the Morning Room, but found she was incapable of eating. Her ears still strained for sounds of masculine voices emerging from the library, and she had scarcely finished her cup of tea when she pushed her plate aside and stood up.

Instinct made her head outdoors. She didn't bother with a jacket, and her feet in their short suede ankle boots were fine for the pathways, even if the dew-wet grass would get them sopping wet. She scrunched rapidly over the gravel, heading for the Italian garden. On the far side of it a paved path led down to a little sunken garden that was always a sun-trap in the morning, with a bowered bench set there for that very purpose. After mopping the ironwork seat dry, with some tissues brought for the purpose, she sat down.

Her eyes gazed blindly over the spring flowers bobbing in the light morning breeze. The leaves of the rose bushes were dark red, still furled. Blossom from the ornamental tree in the centre shone palest pink against the blue sky. The tiny bite of cold she had felt when she first sat down stung and made her shiver.

She was waiting. She knew she was. She was waiting and waiting for it to be safe to go back indoors. And as she waited that same oppressive sense of foreboding stole over her.

Despite the brightness of the spring sunshine, and the warm shelter of the sunken garden, she shivered. Her ears strained for the sound of a car engine starting up, signalling that once more Salton was safe.

There was a footfall on stone. Her head flew up.

Diego Saez had walked into the sunken garden.

CHAPTER SIX

PORTIA had frozen again, he could see, just the way she had last night, when he'd walked into her drawing room. Going completely rigid as only an outraged woman of her class could. It was as if an invisible layer of ice had settled over her whole body.

As he strolled towards her his eyes flicked over her again, taking in the fine bones of her face, the slender wrist, the discreet swell of her breasts beneath the softest cashmere that made him want to hold her in his hands…

But if the thought of caressing her breasts heated him, the look on her face was designed to do just the opposite. Yet the icy disdain in those grey eyes merely acted like a spurt to the anger which he held, like a jaguar on a leash, beneath the surface of his conscious mind.

She had come here to avoid him—she might as well have written it in letters a metre high! Just as she had left the dining table last night and disappeared. Making her aristocratic disdain for him so obvious he'd have had to be a clod of earth not to recognise it. He felt the leashed jaguar growl silently as it crouched, waiting to be given the order to surge forward.

But he would not loose his anger on her. Would not reduce himself to her level—lashing out at him like that, her eyes flashing with contempt for him for all the world to see, dismissing him like some peasant!

No—he stilled the tensing jaguar—he would not loose his anger on her.

He would play a far, far more enjoyable game with her.

* * *

Portia felt ice fill her veins. It was a mix of rage—and dread.

Rage because how dared, how *dare* Diego Saez persecute her like this?

And dread because there was something about the way he was walking towards her, something purposeful in his long, rhythmic stride, that crushed the breath from her lungs.

It did something else too. Something she pushed away blindly, urgently, as if she had suddenly seen a poisonous spider on her bare leg. But not before she had felt its fatal bite. Felt the poison enter her flesh.

Heating it.

She wanted to leap to her feet, wanted to turn on her heel and rush out of the garden, away from him as fast as she could. But the ice filling her veins kept her frozen in position. All she could do was let her fingers clutch at the sides of the cardigan at her throat, as if that might free the choking sensation in her throat.

In a voice as tight as steel she heard herself speak. Sharply. Cuttingly.

'I don't know why you came here but I want you to leave! I have nothing more to say to you!'

He stilled. He was about six feet away from her and seemed to be twice her height. Again she urged herself to stand up, and again realised that it was quite beyond her power.

For one long, paralysing moment he simply went on standing there, looking down at her. He was wearing a business suit, immaculately tailored, and it seemed to make him look taller, darker than ever. His obsidian eyes surveyed her, and she felt the breath stall in her lungs.

'I have something to tell you,' he said, in his deep, accented voice, 'which you would be advised to listen to.'

Her lip curled.

'I can't imagine that there is anything in the world I want to hear you say!'

His face was expressionless. Then, with a slight turn of his head, he indicated the pale gold mass of the house across the lawn rising behind her. Slowly his gaze came back to her, and what she saw in his eyes hollowed her out.

Then, his face still completely expressionless, he spoke.

'If you want to save your precious family home you will listen to every word I have to tell you.'

He had her.

Every synapse in her brain, every nerve in her body, was focused on him. Instantly. Totally.

A cold sense of pleasure went through him. Again, the years split away, and there was Mercedes de Carvello, her black, mascaraed eyes totally focused on him—her disbelief instant, her denial total—as he informed her of the new state of ownership of her home.

Now, in a different place, beneath a different sun, Portia Lanchester, who considered herself too good for his bed, had exactly the same expression in her eyes.

'Are you mad?'

The clipped, upper-class tones cut through the morning air, carrying every gram of her disbelief, her denial.

He looked down at her. Saw the fingers digging into the soft cashmere at her neck. The soft gleam of sunlight on the row of pearls at her throat.

He had a sudden vision of her wearing nothing but those pearls. Walking towards him. Towards his bed. To do there whatever he wanted her to do.

And she would do it. He knew that. Knew it with every fibre of his being.

Knew it because it was what Mercedes de Carvello had done…

He dragged his mind away. He would not remember. Would not remember how the woman who had killed his mother, mown her down like a dog beneath the wheels of her car, had come to him that night he had returned to San

Cristo, his heart heavy despite the cold pleasure of having taken possession, with the full panoply of the law to endorse him, of the *estancia* that had ground his parents into the dirt. Would not remember how she had come to his penthouse suite in the de luxe American hotel in the city, stripping the clothes from her body, offering herself to a man she had thrown from her house as a boy—the house he now owned, the house she was prepared to do anything, *anything* to get back…

He had thrust her from his room, his whole being filled with disgust, with loathing.

But this woman here, now, in front of him, her well-bred chin lifted as if she could smell the dirt of his former poverty in her delicate nostrils—her he would not reject…

What was it, he found himself questioning yet again, that made Portia Lanchester a woman he wanted so badly? She was nothing like his usual women. He had always preferred the voluptuous type—enticing, alluring, fully aware of their own sexuality, and of his.

Portia Lanchester was quite different. He had assessed that instantly, the first time he'd lain eyes on her at that bankers' dinner. She had looked so *apart*. So completely oblivious to the regard she was gathering from male eyes.

Except his.

The memory of how she had realised he was looking her over replayed in his mind, and he savoured the moment, as he had done so often before, when she had met his eyes and recognised in them the look of his desire.

For that briefest moment she had let him look at her, knowing he was looking at her. And then all that chill had flowed back into place, freezing him out.

It hadn't bothered him. It had interested him. Had she returned his assessment with the kind of knowing satisfaction with which women usually received his attentions then he would have been swiftly bored.

But Portia Lanchester had merely made him want her more.

And he would have her.

The desire to possess her was incontrovertible. The more she sought to evade him, the more he knew he was going to possess her.

And the more he wanted her.

Wanted to loosen that fine spun-gold hair and let it cascade over those slender, elegant shoulders. Wanted to reveal those high, soft breasts and feel them harden in his hands. Wanted to skim his hands down over those pale flanks and part her white thighs, take her, possess her.

Her constant evasion of his pursuit had merely made him more determined. He had hunted her down.

And then, like a deer at bay, she had turned on him. Lashed back at him with weapons that had been deadly.

To herself.

Until that moment outside the hotel he would have had infinite patience in his pursuit of her. Relishing every moment, assiduous in his inexorable wearing down of her resistance to him, until the moment came when she finally, gloriously yielded to what he wanted—and found her own satiation in that infinite fount of pleasure which he would release in her.

But at that moment when she had turned on him, rejecting him with words that doomed her, patience had become—unnecessary. He need exert no sensitivity towards her now, no consideration for her reluctance to let him ignite in her the passion that he knew was buried deep within her. Now he need only exert the pressure he knew she would respond to—the pressure that would make her do what all her kind did. Protect her possessions.

And so he would take her. Not against her will. For she would consent to him—consent to the deal he would offer her, the deal that would protect the possessions her kind thought most precious. And she would consent—oh, much more than merely *consent*!—to the pleasures she would find with him. And to make her feel such pleasure, even while her conscious mind would know that she had come to his bed merely to protect her possessions, *that* would assuage his anger.

His anger that a woman who had so beguiled him—so eluded him—had in an instant plunged him back to the sickening memory of the moment when he had taken his revenge on those who had destroyed his family and cast him onto the streets like a dog.

He felt that anger lick at him like black flame and he doused it. He did not need to feel angry with Portia Lanchester for despising him for what he was. He need only desire her—and enjoy her.

He shifted his weight minutely from one leg to the other. At another time he might have enjoyed playing with her a little longer, as a cat with its prey. But, abruptly, he wanted now only to go in for the kill. He would break her arrogance, her aristocratic disdain, with a single blow, as a cat would break the neck of the prey caught in its claws.

He spoke briefly and brusquely, not bothering to soften the blow he aimed at her.

'Your brother has got himself up to his neck in debt—he's put Salton up as security.'

The words fell with killing force.

She heard them, but she didn't hear them. They seemed to come from very far away, and then right up close. For a long, timeless moment she just went on sitting there, ice all the way through her, wondering what it was she had just heard Diego Saez tell her.

Only three words registered—debt, Salton, security.

Then behind the words came a kind of sickness, like some huge, overwhelming tidal wave, engulfing her.

'No—'

Her voice was so faint it was scarcely audible. But he heard it. His face remained expressionless. When he spoke he was merciless.

'Loring Lanchester has become a byword for bad investments. It's sinking faster than a stone in water. Your brother hasn't a hope in hell of dragging it clear. He's put Salton up as security because no one will bail him out. But it won't be enough. It will go. Along with the rest of the bank.'

She stared at him. The obsidian eyes were looking down at her. There was no expression in them—nothing. They might have been the eyes of some Aztec statue—indifferent, blank.

She tried to gather her thoughts, picking them up like bits of paper gusting in the wind. She realised she had got to her feet, but had no conscious memory of doing so. And she still had to look up into those eyes, those dark, shuttered eyes set in that dark, sublime face.

He had just said something so absurd, so ridiculous, that she could not find the words to refute him. As if explaining something to a child, she spoke.

'Mr Saez, I appreciate that you are used to the extreme volatility of the economy of South America, where banks crash and currencies become worthless overnight, but I'm afraid you must appreciate that here in England things are very different. Loring Lanchester is one hundred and fifty years old. It is one of the most highly regarded merchant banks in the City. There can be no question, no question whatsoever, of it being in trouble. Loring Lanchester is one of the soundest, most financially secure—'

'Loring Lanchester is broke.' Diego Saez's voice cut across her clipped tones with harsh brutality.

Something stabbed at Portia. It was fear—a slicing, shearing stab of fear. She thrust it aside.

'Mr Saez, I simply don't think you understand how business is done in this country!' Her voice had risen slightly in pitch. Her hands tightened on the edges of her cardigan.

His face was still blank. For some reason that made the fear slice at her again.

His voice was a dark drawl. 'I understand that when a bank makes loans that are massively defaulted on then it is broke. Loring Lanchester has done just that. Your brother has made a series of disastrous decisions, resulting in a loan portfolio that hasn't a chance in hell of paying out! He's loaned the bank's money to every no-hope venture going—from Eastern Europe to Africa to the most tin-pot banana republic you can name! He'll have to write off just about all of it! And he doesn't even have any income to begin to cover him—the last two years of recession have seen merger and acquisition activity plummet, and bankers' fees with it! M&As may be picking up now, but it's not going to be enough to bail out Loring Lanchester. Nothing can. Your brother has been trawling the City for cash—but no one's about to bail him out. No one! He's going to lose it all. And Salton.'

She was reeling. Reeling as if a hurricane had caught her in its pitiless teeth.

'Salton belongs to Tom outright! It's not part of the bank!'

His eyes flashed derisively.

'You weren't listening, were you? He's already put Salton up as security. It will go with the rest of the bank. The house and estate are just about the only solid assets he's got!'

She shook her head. There was a muzziness in her brain. This wasn't true. This wasn't happening. It couldn't be…

She had to get away. Had to. Had to find Tom. Get him to tell her it wasn't true. That this awful, awful man was simply telling lies—vile, ugly lies. It wasn't true. Wasn't true!

She stumbled away. A hand whipped out, securing her arm.

'I've already told you. There's no point running, Portia.'

His voice was too close. His body was too close. She could smell, with an overpowering sense of nausea, the scent of his aftershave, could feel the crushing presence of his body, too close to hers. She tried to tug away, but she was powerless.

'There's no point,' he said again, and she could feel his

breath on the back of her neck. His other hand reached up and closed over her shoulder. She was held still, almost within the cradle of his arms, but her whole body strained away from him.

'And there's no need to panic the way you're doing. Your brother has found his white knight. The bank is safe.' He paused. 'Salton is safe.'

She should feel relief sagging through her at his words, but she did not. Only the teeth of the hurricane again, biting at her the way Diego Saez's hand was biting around her forearm. She strained away from him.

'Wh—who…?'

She got the word out somehow.

And knew the answer even before he spoke.

She could hear the smile in his voice. Feel the sickening plunge of her heart.

He turned her around so that he could look at her. Look at her hearing what he was going to tell her.

'Why do you think I'm here, Portia? Why do you think your brother brought me here?' He looked down at her, savouring the moment. 'He thinks I'm going to save his skin.'

Time had stopped again. The world was motionless around her. Not even her heart was beating. Her eyes were fixed on his; she felt them spear her. Her voice was a husk.

'And are you?'

It was pointless asking. Because she knew—dear God, she knew what the answer was going to be. What it could only be. Because why else would Diego Saez be here, telling her that her world had just crashed around her ears?

For one purpose. One purpose only.

He went on holding her, looking down at her.

'Of course,' he told her. 'I've thrown him a lifeline. I'll sort out the bank's debts—I'll even let him stay on. It wouldn't be good for the bank right now for him to leave. Martin Loring will have to go, of course—your brother should have cleared him out when he took over. He's the worst liability the bank possesses. If your brother had got rid of him he might have stood a chance. He could have brought in a team of directors who knew one end of a balance sheet from the other! Who could have sold out to one of the global majors for a good price—because then it would have been a profitable deal, not a salvage sale! But your brother let Martin Loring behave as though Queen Victoria were still on the throne and he could order gunships to go in and secure British assets in the world's rough spots!'

Her eyes fell, squeezing shut.

'He wanted Uncle Martin to retire,' she whispered.

'He should have kicked him out on his useless backside! There's no room for sentiment in business, Portia.'

Her eyes flew open and she forced herself to lift them to his again. Her body strained, rigid in his grip.

'So why are you bailing him out?'

It was another pointless question.

And she answered it herself. Her eyes slid past him, out over the little sunken garden, through the archway in the yew hedge at the far side, down the path that wound back along to the lake, which lay like a glittering diamond in the emerald grass of the lawns that lapped around the jewel that was Salton. Her home. Tom's home. It would have been Felicity's home with him, and their children together, and their children's children…

But it would now belong—her heart crushed like a rotten fruit inside her, oozing poisoned bile—to the man who was pinioning her, holding her immobile, powerless.

The man who had looked at the Gainsborough painting of Salton and wanted it there and then. Asked whether it was for sale…

'You want Salton.'

Her voice was dull. Dead.

Her eyes went on gazing. The breeze was moving the branches of the trees beyond the garden, winnowing in the branches of the ornamental tree within it, showering blossom to the ground like a blessing.

She could feel nothing. Nothing at all.

Then, slowly, as if surfacing out of insensibility, she felt something. His hand moving on her shoulder, his fingers stroking the softness of her cashmere.

'No.' His voice was low. Accented.

Her eyes dragged back to his, as if each were bowed with unbearable weight.

She saw what was written there in his eyes, and knew instantly, mortally, just why he had done this. Come to Salton, sought her out, told her that her world had been destroyed.

And he was telling her now, in the depths of those dark, obsidian eyes, just what the price would be to save it.

His hand smoothed over her shoulder again. Hard. Warm. Heavy.

Possessive.

'I want *you*, Portia,' he said.

CHAPTER SEVEN

HER interview with Tom was painful. Agonisingly painful. She had to wait over an hour before seeing him. Diego Saez had walked away from her, there in the little sunken garden where her world had ended, and closeted himself with her brother in the library. Then a chauffeur-driven car had arrived at the front door, a fast, powerful, expensive saloon, and Diego Saez had climbed inside and been driven off.

Portia had given Tom five minutes, then walked indoors.

What had struck her first, like some ghastly bad joke, was that he no longer looked ill.

Ill? The sick humour of it struck at her. Tom hadn't been ill—hadn't been coming down with flu. He'd been sick with worry, with fear! And she'd been blind to it! Totally, completely blind!

Guilt coursed through her. Her own brother, floundering in despair, and she hadn't even noticed.

Yet now, seeing his face clear of that haggard, drawn look only made her lungs squeeze. Because there could be only one reason for Tom no longer looking at death's door.

Diego Saez had offered him his lifeline.

As she stood, hovering on the entrance to the library, he surged towards her.

'Portia! Come in! Listen—I've something I've got to tell you!'

She listened, trying desperately hard to conceal her own emotions, as he poured out to her, at last, the situation at the bank. He was so full of self-recrimination, constantly berating himself for having let it get so bad, excusing everyone but himself, that Portia could not bear it.

Even less could she bear him extolling Diego Saez.

'If he'd ridden up on a white charger I couldn't have been more relieved!' he exclaimed. 'He's giving me the breathing space we need. Oh, he'll take the majority holding—I can hardly expect anything else—but the main thing is that the bank will keep going. He'll sort out the situation, get everything in order, and use his massive financial muscle to knock heads together. He'll get us clean, and then he'll organise an orderly sale to one of the US giants. He's happy to wait to take his profit then, and he will, too—I wouldn't begrudge him a penny of it!'

He frowned slightly. 'Uncle Martin will have to go. I knew he'd insist on that—and if I'd had more gumption myself I'd have done the same. Trouble is—' he looked at his sister wryly '—it's pretty difficult to tell the seventy-year-old man who taught me how to bowl that he's not wanted on voyage any longer. I always knew he lived in the past, but I thought—well, I thought I could carry him.' His face took on a guilty look. 'But I couldn't. And I damn near ruined everything, thinking I could!'

She took an unsteady breath. 'And what about you, Tom? What happens now with you?'

He gave a shaky smile—but at least it was a smile. 'Well, Saez wants me to carry on for a bit—though he'll find a good man to underpin me, and he'll be taking all the decisions. Then, when he thinks the time is right, I'll resign. Yes, I know it's a comedown, but, Portia, for me it's like the end of term! You can't believe how much I've come to loathe that damn bank! And now I'm going to be free of it.'

He made a face and looked her in the eyes. 'I'm going to live here, marry Felicity, look after Salton and be a countryman at last! It's what I've always wanted to do.'

His expression was like that of a reprieved prisoner.

She returned his shaky smile with one even shakier. 'I know. And hearing you say you're definitely going to marry Fliss is brilliant! She's hopelessly in love with you, you know, Tom.'

His eyes shadowed for a moment. 'But till now I couldn't ask her. How could I, when I had all this fiasco hanging over me? But I'm clear now—as soon as Saez takes over and the contracts are signed!'

She swallowed, and forced the words from her.

'When's that going to be?'

'Well, all the paperwork will have to be drawn up first. There's a whole bunch of legal stuff that has to be gone through, and then the banking regulators have to give it all the OK and so on, but it's all just a formality.'

'Can he pull out?' Her voice was sharper than she intended.

Tom shook his head.

'He's got no reason to. He's already gone through the bank's books with a fine-tooth comb, and there's no more bad news to come—he's got the lot! So why would he pull out?'

Why indeed? thought Portia, with a hollowing of her stomach.

She walked across to the window, her stomach roiling. Outside the long library windows the lawns stretched for ever, it seemed to her. And a path stretched before her. Dark, and paved with sharpest glass. It was the path she would have to walk.

She had no choice. None.

Behind her, Tom was speaking. She strained to hear his voice.

'I know this has come as a shock, sis, and I'm really, really sorry. But thank God it's all worked out all right! I was just about suicidal…'

His voice trailed off.

Guilt crushed her. *She* had been distraught at the thought of losing Salton—but for Tom, for her brother, the guilt would have been a hundred times worse! Guilt at having failed to guard his inheritance, which he had been handed on trust for his son, as Salton had been passed, father to son, for nearly half a millennium.

She stared out over the grounds. In every life, she knew, there was a test—an ordeal to be endured.

This was to be hers. The ordeal of knowing that she had no choice. She could not, *could not*, give Diego Saez any reason to pull out from saving her brother. He had made it totally, utterly clear what he wanted. The price he was exacting.

And she would have to pay it.

Her eyes gazed over the sunlit gardens. For her brother's sake she would pay the price that Diego Saez demanded of her.

Whatever it cost her.

A terrible urge to laugh hysterically almost overcame her. She fought it back. From now on she must do everything to suppress her emotions. She must allow herself none.

Because the price she was going to pay to protect Salton was far more costly than even Diego Saez intended her.

For him, taking her to bed was simply a matter of appetite, a passing, easily sated desire. She had defied him, refused him—scorned him. So he had found a way to change her mind. By offering her brother his only chance to save Salton.

He knew she could not refuse. Knew that finally she would now come to him—give him what he wanted. Her body.

He thought he was breaking her pride, her self-respect, but she knew with a terrible sense of foreknowledge that he was going to break something far, far more precious to her. Something that she had known all along would be in the gravest danger if she succumbed to what he wanted from her—a brief, fleeting, meaningless affair. That would be all it was for him. But for her—

She shut her eyes in anguish. Now that she knew she could not escape him, she also knew that she could no longer deny why she had run from him.

Diego Saez was going to take her to his bed—and break her heart into the bargain.

'Mr Saez's suite, please.'

'Certainly, madam. Whom may I say is calling?'

The voice of the hotel clerk was polite, but Portia knew he would insist on a name.

'Portia Lanchester.'

Her own voice was rock-steady. She would allow no tremor in it. None.

She had driven up to London that afternoon, grateful that Tom had told her that as he was at Salton he would stay a while, now that his fears for the bank, for Salton, were put at rest.

'One moment, madam.'

The line went quiet for a few seconds. Then the clerk spoke again. 'Just putting you through now, Ms Lanchester.'

There was a click, and then a strong, masculine voice spoke.

'Portia.' Just her name, that was all.

She felt the constricted passageway of her throat tighten. After all the chasing he had done, now he was going to make her do the running.

'I'm—I'm at my flat. I... I...wondered whether you might be free for dinner tonight.'

She could feel the seconds pass, each one an eternity.

Then down the line came that same voice.

Her fingers clutched at the phone so tightly her nails were white. He gave her her answer.

'I'm flying out tonight, Portia. But if you wish you could come over now.'

Her throat closed completely.

'Now?'

It scraped through her lips, scarcely audible.

'I think so. Don't you?'

The voice was controlled—very controlled—but she

could hear emotion beneath it. It would be satisfaction, she knew. The satisfaction of a rich, spoilt, powerful man who had just achieved what he had wanted.

She put the phone down, feeling a wave of faintness going through her. Was she really going to go through with this? Give herself up to Diego Saez? Take a taxi to his hotel at this hour and…and… *Go to bed with him.* That was what he wanted. He was flying out tonight, and he wanted to make sure he'd had his before he went. After all, who knew when a busy international financier like him would be back in London again?

A shiver went through her. Would Diego Saez expect her to be waiting for him when he came back to London, whenever that was? Was she supposed to be his woman in London for the time being?

Stop it! She tore her mind away. What was the point of tormenting herself like this? Didn't she have enough to feel anguished about? Tom was in danger of losing Salton—and the only lifeline being held out to him was Diego Saez's.

And it came with a condition.

She was going to have to put aside all her principles about not indulging in a brief, physical affair with a man whose attitude to women, to sex was abhorrent to her.

A word came into her mind, ugly and vile.

Was she *prostituting* herself? To save Salton for her brother?

A bitter expression lit her eyes. What did it matter what you called it? She could not—could not—let Tom lose Salton just because she did not want an affair with Diego Saez. A man who with a single look could make her tremble...

A deep, abiding sense of inevitability swept through her. She had run all she could, denied him and defied him, scorned him and condemned him. But it had all been in vain.

Diego Saez would possess her, enjoy her, and dispose of

her. What she had most feared, most fled from, would happen, after all.

She had no choice.

Slowly she walked into her bedroom and started to get changed. To adorn herself for Diego Saez.

Diego stood by the window of his penthouse suite and gazed out over the traffic on Park Lane and across to the dark mass of Hyde Park beyond. Through the soundproofed windows the roar of the traffic was silent, the endless procession of red tail-lights and white headlights streaming along the busy road.

His mind slipped away to another city.

Another time.

The stench. That was what he remembered most about San Cristo. The stench of poverty, destitution, despair. The stifling heat of the day and the chill of the nights as he lay, arms crossed over and hands tucked into his armpits, knees drawn up, sleeping in filthy doorways, with the perpetual gnaw of hunger in his belly.

And blackness in his soul.

Like a shutter, he closed the past away from him and turned away from the window. He never allowed himself to remember. Never.

All he ever allowed himself to do was send money to Father Tomaso, who spent his life gathering up the unwanted street children, day after day, little by little earning their trust, reaching out to them until they turned to him and came with him to the refuge he offered them. Shining the first ray of light into their unbearably dark lives.

Now, thanks to money from the Saez coffers, more and more street children could be taken into refuge, given the chance that he had been given so long ago to become something other than human detritus thrown away on the midden of unspeakable poverty—as he had been, before Father Tomaso had found him and rescued him.

Deliberately he summoned another memory, a far more

recent one, to replace the dark horror that lay haunting him, deep within his mind. As he crossed the room on long legs, heading for the drinks cabinet, he saw in his mind's eye the stately proportions of the dining room at Salton—two hundred and fifty years of gracious living, frozen in time. His expression hardened. How could anyone born to that have been so careless with it? Tom Lanchester was a fool. It had taken a single glance at the bank's books for him to know that. Still, he should be glad of it. After all, thanks to Lanchester's financial idiocy he now had within his reach something that he intended to possess to the full.

He poured a shot of whisky into a glass, feeling his body enter that most pleasurable state of imminent sexual arousal. She would be here soon.

Another memory slid into his mind, mingling with the sensations beginning to stir in his body. Portia Lanchester, wearing that classy, understated black number last night as he'd walked into her ancestral home. It had been her face he'd concentrated on, relishing the expression of outraged disbelief on her well-bred features, but it had not blinded him to her body. The material of the dress had been silky, but slightly stretchy, grazing her breasts and outlining the delicate sculpture of her shoulders. Her pearls had leant their sheen to her skin, giving it a translucence that had been almost tangible.

What would she be wearing when she came to him now? As he lifted the whisky glass to his mouth he found himself hoping that she would not signal her intentions too obviously. She would come, of course, to offer him her body in exchange for safeguarding her family's wealth—and he would, of course, accept her offer. But he did not want her to do so dressed for that role.

The glass stilled at his lips, and he found himself lowering it slowly. Something moved in his mind. Some emotion. He wondered what it was, and then he realised.

It was regret.

His eyes darkened minutely.

Regret, he knew, that his pursuit of Portia Lanchester should end in this fashion.

It was not what he had intended.

He had intended a quite different affair. One in which Portia Lanchester succumbed to his desire for him simply because—

Because all women he desired did so.

He cast his mind around. Had there ever been a woman who had resisted his desire for her? He could remember none. He had only to indicate his interest and she was his. Nor was it just his wealth that made them so responsive. All his life, even while clawing his way out of poverty, women had come easily to him.

Except Portia Lanchester.

That, of course, had been part of her allure—that she had resisted him.

A frown entered his darkening eye.

But she had gone on resisting him, and allure had begun to turn to impatience. So he had called time. And then—his mouth tightened into a grim line—she had revealed the reason for her resistance outside Claridge's.

Her contempt for his origins.

Dismissing him as not worthy of her illustrious breeding and ancestry.

Not good enough for her.

And in that instant the game had changed.

He lifted the whisky glass to his lips and took a generous mouthful, letting the complex fiery liquid burn around his palette, savouring the sensation.

Portia Lanchester had changed the game, and now it was being played out with new rules. She had made clear her values to him—all that was important to her was her money and her social status. To protect that she would do whatever she had to.

Including coming to his bed.

Slowly Diego let the whisky glide down his throat, kicking into his system. It felt good. His body felt taut, and fit, the first tightening of sexual anticipation was tensing through him.

He glanced at his watch. The gold gleamed in the lamplight.

She would be here soon.

He took another mouthful of whisky, and waited.

He had waited a long time for Portia Lanchester.

But soon, very soon, the waiting would be over.

Portia could hear her heels click on the marble floor of the luxury hotel fronting Park Lane. Once the site had been the lavish townhouse of an aristocratic family, torn down after the First World War to be replaced by an even more lavish art deco luxury hotel. Park Lane was lined by such hotels, from Marble Arch to Hyde Park Corner.

The one that Diego Saez patronised was one of the very best—in fact, one of the best hotels in the world. Well, for a man of his wealth—who could afford to buy a failing bank just to make sure of a woman he wanted—the outrageous cost of a suite here would be negligible.

She reached the front desk.

'Mr Saez's suite, please,' she announced.

If there was a tremor in her voice she would not acknowledge it. She stood, poised and elegant, in a pale blue cocktail dress just right for this early hour of the evening. In the tea lounge opening off the main lobby she could hear a grand piano playing quietly. Chopin, she recognised absently.

She listened to the nocturne as the reception clerk phoned up to Diego Saez's suite, then, a moment later, a bellboy was hovering attentively, ready to show her up.

She felt strange. Frozen somehow. Dissociated. As if none of this were real. For a moment, as she stepped out of the lift and the bellboy went ahead to rap on the door of the suite, she could not even remember what Diego Saez looked like.

Then the door opened and he was there.

She walked in.

Behind her, Diego Saez pressed the requisite note into the bellboy's hand and closed the door. It closed silently, with only the barest click.

It was a very final click.

Somewhere deep, deep inside her, she felt her heart begin to thud.

Diego Saez let his eyes rest on the woman who had come to him, as he had known she would, to offer him her body in exchange for her family's wealth. A sense of satisfaction went through him. She looked exactly the way he wanted her to look. She had resisted the temptation to come on too obviously to him, by wearing some seductive, sexy number. Instead she was wearing a dress that was the very opposite of that.

It was the colour of pale water, very plain, but beautifully cut, gliding over her fine-boned body, revealing nothing, baring only her arms. Her hair was dressed exactly the way he liked it. A low, elegant chignon nested at the nape of her neck, the hair swept back from her face, exposing her sculpted features, her wide-set grey eyes. She had used minimum make-up, and he liked that too. It was subtle, like the scent she wore. In fact, he mused, he doubted she was wearing perfume at all. The fragrance was so faint it was probably just soap and face cream.

Her lipstick was barely there, just a slight gloss, and there was nothing more than a sweep of mascara and the merest hint of shadow to deepen her eyes. There was no foundation or powder on her flawless skin.

He went on looking at her, taking in her whole appearance—from her freshly washed hair, down over her slender body to the cool blue material of her dress, down her slim legs to her small feet in modestly heeled shoes that exactly matched the colour of the dress.

She looked exactly what she was. A woman born into a world of Old Masters and vintage port, of landed estates and old money, of heritage and bloodlines—privileged, protected.

Protected from men like him.

His eyes rested on her, and for an instant so brief it was hardly there darkness clouded his gaze. Then it was gone.

Instead, he turned his mind to the physical sensations that had been releasing slowly inside him as he had looked at her.

She looked as cool, as untouchable as white marble. He felt his body surge. He had waited for her for so long—far longer than any other woman he'd wanted—and now, finally, she was here.

That pang he had felt earlier came again. For an instant, like a blade on his skin, he felt regret that it should be on terms such as this.

Then he put the thought aside. She could despise his lowly origins all she liked, but if she wanted to save her precious family home she would overcome her revulsion to him.

Something burned briefly in his eyes. Oh, yes, she would overcome her revulsion, all right. Portia Lanchester would enjoy every moment of her time in his bed…

He would make sure of that.

It was as if she had stepped into an abyss.

Yet it was very strange. She was not falling. Instead she seemed to be sort of held motionless, as if suspended. She could feel nothing. There was nothing to feel. Diego Saez was there. He was looking at her. The way he always looked at her.

Up to now she had always felt oppressed whenever he looked at her. Felt haunted, hunted. She had wanted to get away, to escape from that gaze that rested on her, dark, assessing, *knowing*.

Wanting her.

Yet now, when she was here, standing in front of him,

knowing that she had fled from in vain, it was as if a fine film of ice had formed all over her.

With part of her mind she realised it was a form of self-protection. She thought back to the first time she had seen Diego Saez's dark, knowing eyes resting on her. Making her aware, as she had never been so aware in her life, of her own body.

Yet now she felt as if she were almost a ghost. Or an inanimate statue. As if her blood were suspended in her veins.

The reality of what she was doing opened up around her. She had come to Diego Saez—now he would take the clothes from her body, take her to his bed, make her his own.

She knew it, but she could not believe it. It was so unreal, surreal.

Her eyes went to the huge formal arrangement of flowers on a gilded pier table across the wide reception room of the suite in which she now stood so motionless. The exotic scented blooms were like those he had sent her—a million years ago, it seemed—that morning after the bankers' dinner.

Did I think then it would come to this?

No—how could she have?

And yet—

Deep inside her there came a sense of inevitability about what was happening. It went through every fibre of her being. It was as if, right from that first moment when her gaze had intersected his, this moment had been waiting for her.

Dispassionately she stood still, let herself be looked at.

Suspended, immobile. And quite, quite passive.

When he finally spoke she turned her face slightly to look at him.

And as she did so she felt a shaft of emotion pierce her. She could not name it, only feel it.

It was powerful, overwhelmingly powerful. It knifed

through her, slicing through the blankness, making it suddenly, instantly non-existent.

Her eyes met his. Out of his poured something that was almost tangible, as if it were streaming over her, touching every pore of her body.

It possessed her, possessed her utterly.

The knifing, overwhelming emotion came again, and for a long, endless moment it occupied her totally, as if there was nothing else inside her.

Except the touch of his eyes.

'So, tell me, Portia—what is it you want?'

His voice was low, with the deep, accented timbre that seemed to resonate through her body.

Want? The word seemed to mock her.

She dragged her eyes from him as if she were caught in a force field, a vortex, and hauled them back to the vase of flowers in their ornate vase. Safe from that sucking, knifing emotion that had possessed her when she experienced the touch of his eyes.

She took a breath. The air seemed cold in her lungs. Chill.

'I want Salton to be safe.'

Again her eyes met his, but this time she was better prepared. The knifing sensation came again, but she was expecting it. She let it pass through her body and then empty out again.

'And is that all you want?' Something had fired in the depths of those dark eyes, but she could give no name to it.

She could not answer him.

She turned her head away, walking towards the vase of flowers. She seemed so calm still, and yet inside her something was happening to her that was not calm at all.

She stopped, and reached out her free hand to touch one of the petals. It was heavy and waxy to her touch. There was a mirror behind the vase, and she could see, although she was not looking directly into it, that Diego Saez was walking towards her.

He stood behind her. She did not lift her eyes from the flower, nor move her hand. Only when she felt his hand curve around the nape of her neck did she still completely. Her finger touching the petal hovered immobile, her unvarnished nail gleaming pale against the vivid magenta of the bloom.

But the flowers had disappeared.

The whole world had disappeared.

Only one thing still existed.

The touch at the nape of her neck.

His hand was warm, encircling, resting on the bared skin beneath her chignon. She could feel the tips of his fingers, moving slowly, exploratively, hardly at all. With such a slight movement, how could they engender such sensation?

Because sensation *was* dissolving through her, wave after slow wave, shimmering down her spine, fanning out across her shoulders, easing along her neck, her throat.

She could not move, only stand there as still as a statue while the press of his hand on her nape, the slow moving of the tips of his fingers, became the whole world of existence to her.

Was she still breathing? She did not know. Knew only that the world had become focused minutely, consumingly, on his touch.

The tips of his fingers reached further, spreading out to splay around her throat. His thumb found the small hollow behind her ear, stroking into it gently, so gently, that she thought she must faint and fall, as the shimmering sensation became focused on that one point of being.

Then it shifted, and his thumb and forefinger closed over the tender lobe of her ear, feeling the fullness of that delicate flesh. Slowly, so slowly, she felt her head droop and turn, so that his long fingers could span further, stroke yet more of her throat, while his thumb feathered at the softness of her earlobe.

It seemed to last an eternity. An eternity that dissolved around her as she stood helpless, immobile, while Diego Saez touched her, stroked her. She had no will left, no strength, no resistance.

She was nothing, nothing except sensation. Slow, drugging sensation.

Slowly, as if it were infinitely heavy, she lifted her head to let her eyes gaze ahead. Through the mesh of vivid petals she saw her own reflection, a pale, slight figure, and behind her, as if caging her, Diego Saez's tall, imprisoning darkness.

She stared, eyes unblinking. His hand was still at her neck, but it was motionless now, merely holding the base of her head, watching her watching herself—and him.

Her gaze moved away from herself, shadowed by him, and moved to meet his.

For one eternal moment he held her gaze in the glass, his eyes dark, and hooded, and unreadable.

She felt her lungs tighten. For the briefest instant an urge so great she thought it must overwhelm her shook silently within her.

She should have run. Because if she did not, if she did not run now, something terrible would happen—something that would cost her more than she could pay.

More logic sliced through her mind.

You can't run. If you run now Salton will be lost, your family destroyed. You will have to live with that all your life, the fact that you ran and Salton was lost.

What did she count for compared with that? Whatever price she paid, Salton would be saved—for Tom, for his sons, for his grandsons.

She could not run. Could do nothing—nothing except go on standing here, caged by the man she was going to yield her body to, the man who was already putting his mark on her, with his hand resting on her bared skin.

So it was with complete, absolute acquiescence that without a word, with only the sliding of his hand down over her shoulder, pressing her around, she turned away from the mirror, trailing her fingers away from the vivid waxy petals. And with that same acquiescence she let him guide her forward, his hand splayed now across the small of her back, hardly touching her, but for all that controlling her—totally.

The bedroom was vast, and as opulent as the reception room. The floor-length curtains were already drawn, bedside lights already lit and turned low. She walked into the room, and halted.

Her heart slewed in her chest with heavy, uneven strokes.

He shut the door behind them, then came up to her.

He touched her hair with his hands. Not stroking, simply drawing his fingers lightly back from her temples. That same quivering sensation that had shivered through her when he had touched her nape, her earlobe, her throat, shimmered through her again.

His hands were cupping her chignon now, drawing out one by one the pins that held it. He let them fall to the floor, indifferent to their fate. Long fingers loosened her hair, threading through it until the coils unwound and layered down her back.

Something was happening to her. It was that same sensation again but more, like tiny ripples of water, merging together into larger ripples.

He was speaking—indistinct words. It was Spanish, but none that she could understand. His voice was low. There was a husk in it. She could feel his breath softly on her neck. He had moved the heavy fall of her hair to one side, smoothing it across the material of her dress.

His fingers were at the top of her zip, and with a sudden swift glide he pulled it down the length of her spine, using both hands to part the material. His hands were flat on her bare shoulderblades. The heat in them burned like a brand.

He is branding me. Branding me as his possession.

She felt the breath rise in her throat. The ripples were spreading, growing more and more. Quickening.

The tips of his fingers threaded under the straps of her bra and she realised that not only was the zip of her dress undone, but the clasp of her bra as well. Silently he pushed the material of her dress, the straps of her bra, down over the cusp of her shoulder.

Then, with the same pressure on her shoulders, he turned her around to face him.

She lifted her eyes to him.

His were narrowed, lit with a dark intensity that seemed to pierce her, deep and penetrating.

Again that slicing sensation knifed through her, but now it was a thousand times more potent.

He lifted a hand from her shoulder, and lightly, very lightly, ran the backs of his fingers down her cheek.

She felt weakness flood through her, and that shimmering, shivering sensation again. But she couldn't move. Was trapped utterly in the rippling, emotions cascading through her.

She went on gazing at him, unable to move. Helpless. Helpless with sensation.

Slowly, very slowly, she watched his mouth lower to hers.

She tasted of cool water on a hot day, like scented nectar. He opened her mouth and drank deep from the sweet well.

She did not respond, simply stood there as passive as she had been as he'd stroked her, and for an instant a biting emotion went through him. A low, viscous anger.

Did she really think that she could simply offer him her body as if she were a puppet? Did she really think that she could stay *uninvolved* while she bought her precious stately home for the price of her body in his lowly hands?

Those hands pressed against the bare skin of her back, folding her into him. His kiss deepened.

For an instant, a moment longer, she still resisted him, and then, as if every bone in her body had suddenly melted, she responded.

Triumph surged through him! She could *not* stay uninvolved! No, she would be trembling in his arms, clinging to him—*aching* for him, for his possession!

And he would possess her all right! *Dios*, but he would possess her. She would be his—entirely, consumingly.

He tasted her mouth one last time, then drew back.

He wanted to see all of her.

Portia was drowning, drowning in sensation. The ripples which had been widening suddenly swirled into a white whirlpool, sucking her down.

For an instant, when he had first bent to kiss her, she had felt paralysed, her heart surging into her throat. And then as his kiss deepened the whirlpool of sensation had flooded through her.

He was kissing her as she had never, ever been kissed before. She had never responded like this before. The kiss he had given her at the art gallery had been as a gentle stream. This was a drowning whirlpool, extinguishing everything around her. Nothing else existed except the touch of his lips, his tongue.

And then, just as suddenly, when time had stopped and all meaning, his mouth moved from hers.

She felt bereft, as if she had lost something infinitely precious.

But even as the sense of loss washed through her a new realisation took its place.

He was stripping her.

She could feel the material of her dress slip from her shoulders, taking her loosened bra straps with it, and then suddenly, shockingly, she felt her breasts engorge, her nipples harden.

Slowly, seductively, he slid the dress down her arms. The touch of his hands moving over her bare skin ignited another intense sensation that shimmered through her again. She sought to still it, but it was beyond her power. Everything was beyond her power—except to yield to the exquisite, magical feelings that were rippling through her body.

But as she felt the dress slip completely from her, her bra tumbling to the floor, revealing the swell of her breasts, instinctively, protectively, she shut her eyes.

Immediately she felt the stroke of the backs of his fingers along her cheek. His voice as he spoke was low, commanding.

'Oh, no, Portia—not that way. *This* way—'

She felt the trail of his fingers glide downwards, softly knuckling the line of her throat, and then continue to descend. Softly, very softly, he stroked the side of her breast.

The breath stopped in her throat. He repeated the movement, and this time he brought his other hand to her other breast, stroking outward and downward from the topmost swell of each engorged orb.

The world disappeared. Disappeared completely, utterly. Just as it had when he had stroked along the nape of her neck, so now the entire world simply became the touch of his hands at her breasts.

Sensation dissolved through her.

Her body dissolved.

Into a feeling and emotion she had never, ever in her life felt before. Had never even known existed.

Wonder took over. How, *how* could such feeling exist? Her drawn-down lashes quivered on her cheeks and she gave herself to his soft, exquisite exploration.

She thought she heard Diego Saez say something, but she paid no attention. Her whole being was focused, unseeing, on what she was feeling. That soft, feathering touch, she realised in confusion, was making her breasts feel so strange, so heavy. An extraordinary lassitude was sweeping through her. She felt weak, boneless—his.

She gave a low, helpless moan, deep in her throat.

Her breasts were just as he had wanted them to be. High and pale, with a soft swell to them peaked by small pink tips. As he stroked them to ripening fullness, watching the nipples tighten, he felt his own body echo that hardening in response.

She was giving that low, helpless moan again, her eyes still shut, lashes like silk against her flushed cheeks. Satisfaction scythed through him. Portia Lanchester might not have wanted to soil her fine, aristocratic hands on him, but she was responding to him all the same—completely.

He had known she would. Known from the moment her bored gaze had been speared by his the first time he had set eyes on her, known from the way her body had tensed, signalling its awareness of him, that she would be helpless against him.

Now the pleasure he felt in her response to his touch was more than sensual, lending an edge to his possession of her that quickened his appetite.

He stroked her breasts again, hearing again that soft, blind, helpless moan.

It pleased him, pleased him very much, but he wanted more. Much, much more.

He wanted her naked.

And more—much more.

His hands slid down her silky flanks, feeling the slenderness of her body. As he did so he pushed down the fabric of her dress until it slithered free over her hips and cascaded to the carpet. He rested his hands on her, splaying his fingers around her soft curves.

He looked down at her. Her eyes had opened, and they were staring, wide, dilated, up at him.

For a moment, just a brief, fleeting moment, an emotion jerked through him that had nothing to do with the powerful, throbbing urgency of his state of arousal, nothing to do with the low anger banked down inside him.

It had everything to do with the expression of helpless, wondering vulnerability in her wide grey eyes.

Then, as the needs of his own body surged again, he felt his hands tighten over her hips. And Portia was lost, lost—in a world so wonderful she never wanted to leave.

He scooped her up and carried her to the bed.

CHAPTER EIGHT

THE low throb of the jet engines seemed to vibrate through every cell in Portia's body. She shifted slightly in the wide leather seat.

It did no good.

Her whole body throbbed.

But not because of the vibration from the powerful engines.

She pressed her eyelids shut more tightly, trying to blot out memories as she blotted out vision.

But she could not.

Her body was one entire sensate memory. Every centimetre of her skin bore its imprint. Even the most intimate folds of her body.

Especially those.

Between her thighs the low, insistent throbbing was witness to her folly.

How could I? How could I have responded to him like that?

The rhetorical question mocked her. She knew exactly how—why—she had responded as she had. Because she had been taken somewhere she had not even known existed—an exquisite, ecstatic place of wonder, of enchantment and mystery, a revelation so intense it had transfigured her.

And the person who had taken her there, step by shivering step, had been Diego Saez.

He had lowered her down onto the bed, peeling away the rest of her clothes and then doing likewise with his own. Her eyes had been dazed in wonder when she'd seen his strong, planed body emerge from the dark veneer of his suit.

Geoffrey's body had been slim, almost boyish. There was nothing boyish about Diego Saez's body. Broad shoulders, powerful chest, muscles smooth and gleaming. She had wanted to graze her hands over them, feel their strength, their power. Her arms had reached up to him, touching almost with fear, with wonder, with the tentative tips of her fingers, the contours of his shoulders, his arms.

He had folded down on her, his weight so heavy that she had almost gasped, and then the gasp had turned to a moan as with shock, with piercing pleasure, he had lowered his head to suckle her.

From that moment on she had been lost, utterly carried away on a tide so strong, so irresistible, she had been able to do nothing but be sucked into the white swirling maelstrom of sensation. No part of her body had been secret to him. He had explored, caressed, *possessed* every part of it. And she had lain beneath him, helpless, swept away by what he was doing to her. Time had lost all meaning. Reality had slid away. All that had been real was her body—and what he was doing to it.

It had been a revelation, a miracle. She had never *known* that she could feel like that, feel such hunger, such wonder—such gasping pleasure. Her body had been hers no longer. It had belonged to him, totally to him, the man who had consumed her, possessed her.

And she had been his. She had given herself to him without restraint, without caution—with a yearning, straining ardour that he had drawn from her with every caress, every skilled, arousing touch, until she had been a mesh of sensation.

And when he had possessed her fully, powerfully, surging within her with all his strength, she had gasped at the wonder, the pleasure of it all, exploding all through her again and again.

But that was nothing—nothing to what she had gone on

to feel as, stroke by powerful stroke, he had brought her inexorably, relentlessly to the topmost peak. And then out of nowhere, it seemed—for she had not known her body was capable of it—she had been convulsing around him, crying out, a tide of ecstasy engulfing her in wave after wave of pounding, threshing pleasure.

It had gone on, as if it would never stop, *could* never stop, as if she were one entire fusion of endless, endless bliss.

She had cried out his name, helpless with wanting, with wonder, then cried it out again, wrapping herself around him, holding him to her, because she would never let him go, never…

And then, as she had come down from her ecstasy, her eyes blind, her vision slowly clearing, she had gazed, weak, panting up at him.

He had been looking down at her, shock in his eyes.

She had reached a trembling hand to cup his face.

'Diego...'

Her voice had been a whisper, a last caress.

For an instant longer he had stayed, with her hand curved around his jaw, and then suddenly, as if a bullet had been fired, he'd pulled free from her, put her from him and risen from the bed.

He had walked to the bathroom, and she had seen the play of muscle and sinew in his powerful, sculpted back, had felt again for one fragile, fleeting moment the wonder that had consumed her, and then, at the door to the *en suite* bathroom, he had turned, glancing back at her, his expression blank, indifferent.

'Use the other bathroom, Portia. And then get dressed. Be ready in fifteen minutes—don't keep me waiting.'

Then he had shut the bathroom door.

And in that moment, that sickening, hideous moment, she had realised with punishing, brutal clarity just *why* she had always run from Diego Saez…

Shame had burned through her. Hot, coruscating shame at her own blind, unforgivable folly.

That feeling was with her still now, as she sat, silent and strained, in the first-class airline seat.

And the same question burned through her mind, round and round.

How—how could I have responded to him like that?

To her, the experience had been wondrous, magical. A revelation so exquisite that she had been consumed by it.

To Diego Saez it had been nothing more than a quick lay with a woman he'd had to blackmail into bed with him…

And when it was over, he was done with her.

Until the next time he wanted sex.

Tightness garrotted her throat as she sat in the plane, feeling the low, betraying throb of her flesh, hating herself.

Desperately, brokenly, she had gathered to her the only armour that she had been able to find, like tattered rags to cover her shaming nakedness. And by the time she had walked out into the reception room of the suite, showered and reclothed, her hair redressed in its chignon, only the faint stain of colour along her cheeks and her swollen lips to betray what her state had been such a short time earlier, she had donned that armour, her only frail defence

He'd been standing at the table, immaculately attired in a dark business suit, freshly shaved, white cuffs gleaming against his tanned skin. He'd been closing down his laptop, clicking down the lid and zipping up the case with swift, decisive movements.

Something had gone through her as she'd watched his tall, powerful frame.

She had crushed it down.

It had no place in what had been between them.

He'd turned round.

His face had been shuttered, the way it had been when he'd walked into Salton.

'We'll stop off at your flat on the way. You can pick up

your night things and your passport. Don't take long. The flight won't wait.'

She'd stared.

'Flight? I...I don't understand.'

His mouth had tightened.

'You're coming to Singapore with me.'

'*Singapore*? But—but I—'

He walked to the door and opened it, pointedly waiting for her to walk through.

She took a breath.

'I have a job,' she said in a clipped voice. 'I can't just go...go off to Singapore!'

'You swan off from your job whenever you want,' he replied dismissively. 'Geneva—Yorkshire—America.'

'But that's for my work!'

'And when you disappear down to Salton?'

Her face tightened. 'I have leave owing to me.'

He looked at her impassively. His face was as closed as a book.

'Take some leave now.'

'But—'

He lifted a hand. 'Portia. Save the debate. I'm a busy man. I have more to do in my life than bail out third-rate merchant banks in exchange for sexual favours.'

She whitened like chalk, the breath freezing in her throat.

For a second, so brief she did not see it, something changed in his eyes. Then it was gone.

'I'm flying out to Singapore tonight, Portia. You come with me—you don't come with me. It's your choice.'

His voice was flat. His face expressionless.

So was hers as she walked out of the suite in his wake.

Choice? The word mocked at her, just the way Diego Saez had mocked her with it. She had no choice. If she walked away from him now, when he had indicated that he wanted her to come to Singapore with him, for when he wanted sex again, would he go ahead with his bail-out of

Loring Lanchester? Would Tom lose Salton, everything that meant anything to him?

No, she had no choice. No choice.

She barely had time to collect her passport from her bureau, throw together a small hand valise of essentials, and leave voicemails for Hugh and Tom to say that she had gone abroad at short notice. She did not specify her destination. It was not Hugh's concern—only that she was high-handedly helping herself to yet more leave—and as for Tom…what could she possibly say?

Diego Saez's brutal words seared in her mind—*I have more to do in my life than bail out third-rate merchant banks in exchange for sexual favours…*

Cold flushed through her.

And when Diego Saez has had his fill of you—he'll leave.

Her mind sheered away. She must not think of that. Must not feel. From now on her only salvation was that frail armour she had donned.

She wore it now, as she sat beside him, separated only by the inset drinks table between their seats. He was working, rapidly scanning through dossiers, papers, making marks every now and then with a gold fountain pen. He was utterly self-contained. He had spoken to her only when necessary, in a terse, closed voice. She had done what he had told her—silently, obediently.

A heavy numbness descended over her. The throb of the engines resonated with the throb of her body as the plane ate through the night towards the eastern dawn. She turned her head to stare out of the dark porthole. No stars, no moon visible. Only blackness.

All around her.

It was the late afternoon of the following day when the plane landed at Changi Airport. By the time the chauffeured limo pulled in under the portico of the *de luxe* hotel on Orchard Road the tropical night was already curtained around them, pierced by the jewelled brightness of the city lights. For a few brief moments as she exited the car Portia felt the heat and humidity close over her like a steam bath. The air felt thick to breathe, filling her lungs with warm dampness. But when she walked into the chill of the air-conditioned lobby the cold made her shiver. Or something did.

She walked beside Diego, his long stride making it hard for her to keep up with him. Her feet felt swollen from the long flight, her shoes tight, and she longed for a shower.

She felt dazed, disorientated. Her body clock was completely awry. But even without the time difference she would have felt the same.

If she had thought the suite Diego Saez had occupied in London luxurious, she had to reclassify the one they were shown to now. It was vast—the size of an apartment in its own right. Instinctively she crossed to the huge window. One of the staff was there before her, bowing and asking if she would like to go out on to the terrace. She shook her head and turned back.

Awaiting orders.

Inside her, sickness ate like acid.

Diego disposed of the hovering staff and looked across at Portia Lanchester.

She was as white as a ghost.

His mouth tightened.

'Go and lie down before you pass out.'

His voice sounded brusquer than he'd meant it to.

She seemed to flicker slightly, like a candle guttering before it went out, then, recovering, she looked around, clearly wondering which direction to go in.

'Take the second room. Get some sleep.'

He saw her tense visibly, and the movement irritated him. As she moved past him towards the door he indicated he caught her arm. She stilled utterly, going rigid. He stepped up to her.

'Don't start, Portia, what you aren't prepared to finish,' he said softly.

Then he let her go.

He watched her go into the second room. Then, abruptly, he turned and headed for the terrace.

As he stepped out from the air-conditioned interior of the room the heat enveloped him like a hot, sultry blanket. His breath caught. His hands closed over the warm surface of the balustrade. He stared out into the tropical night.

Memory drenched through him.

The thickness of the air, the instant sweating of the body, the enveloping, encompassing heat. But here, at least, in this clean, hygienic city on the equator, there was no stench—no foetid reek of drains and sewage and contaminated water, of rubbish rotting in the heat, infested with vermin, picked over by the human detritus searching for anything to keep them going in the hell in which they lived out their lives.

His knuckles whitened as they pressed the top of the railings, his shoulders tensing.

Why the hell was he thinking of that stinking cesspool of a slum in San Cristo? He never allowed himself to remember. Never.

But these days the memories intruded more and more. He knew why. He gave a tight, savage smile.

Portia Lanchester. Portia Lanchester with her white skin and her fine bones and her wide, cool grey eyes.

She was opening that gate to the past that he had thought locked for ever.

Portia.

He didn't want to think about her.

The smile vanished, replaced by a closed, forbidding expression.

What the hell had gone wrong?

His stared out into the hot, jewelled night, oblivious to the noise of traffic coming up to him over the tops of the ornamental trees in the hotel grounds.

Portia Lanchester had thought she could offer up her pale, soft body and then get up from his bed without a hair out of place in her chignon!

He had showed her otherwise. *Por Dios*, but he had shown her!

He had wanted her pleading for him—and he'd got what he'd wanted. She'd lain beneath him, hair loosened and tangled on the pillow, eyes wide, dilated, giving those low, moaning gasps in her throat, her straining body arching up to him.

He felt his body tightening even as memory swarmed in his head.

And when she'd come—

Cristos—it had been her first time! It had to have been The shock on her face had been absolute. She had stared up at him incredulous, disbelieving, for one brief second, before orgasm had convulsed through her. She had cried out—a high-pitched sound of anguish and ecstasy—and in that instant, that fraction of a second, it had all gone totally, terrifyingly wrong.

His own body had flooded with her.

A sharp intake of breath knifed through him as he stared blindly out into the dark.

How could it have happened?

He'd been totally, completely, out of control. Unable to halt that sudden, unstoppable surging of his body. The total, absolute need to fill her.

Become one with her.

Roughly he pushed away from the balustrade and strode back inside.

I should have left her in London.

A mocking smile parted his lips. He knew exactly what he'd brought her to Singapore for. Portia Lanchester had sold herself to him, and he was still in the mood to buy her wares.

And next time he took her he would be in total, absolute control.

* * *

The sun was high when she woke. For a good half an hour she just simply lay there, unwilling to go out of her bedroom in case Diego Saez was there. But eventually she realised she couldn't just go on hiding for ever in her room.

Dressing was simple. She'd managed to grab a single sundress and a change of underwear from her flat, and, after her shower, she put them on.

Heart in her mouth, she went out into the suite's sitting room.

It was deserted.

Clutching her handbag, she went out. She had no key, but assumed that the hotel would let her back in if need be.

There was a coffee shop downstairs, off the huge lobby, and she sat there a while, sipping coffee and nibbling a pastry. She didn't feel hungry.

She didn't feel anything.

That total sense of blankness had descended on her again. She could feel nothing.

Deliberately she kept it that way. It was the only way she was going to survive this. She knew that. By keeping that frail armour around her. By recognising, admitting, that there was nothing else for her to do. She had no choice any more. She was here to save Salton—not herself.

And to do that she had to be what Diego Saez wanted her to be.

A body for his bed.

Nothing more.

And when she was not in his bed, then she would have to keep that frail armour around her—the armour that kept the rest of the world away from her, kept her within a blank, insensate cocoon.

It was the only way to get through.

She paid for her breakfast with her credit card, and wandered out into the lobby again. Outside, through the revolving doors, she could see hot sunshine beating down.

She wondered what to do. Presumably she ought to stay in the hotel.

And do what?

The place must have a pool, she supposed, and went across to the desk to make enquiries. The smiling assistant also indicated the small interior mall of shops and boutiques, stretching in a wide corridor beyond the bank of lifts. Using her credit card again, Portia bought herself a swimsuit. It was not her usual style, but it came with a filmy sarong in a matching gold and turquoise print.

Even through the shade of a thick parasol Portia could feel the sun beating down on her back. She would need to cool off in the pool again, but right now she was too tired to move. Although she'd slept till late she still felt exhausted.

It must be the heat...

But it was more than exhaustion of the body, she knew, even after the long, unexpected flight and the change in time-zones.

It was exhaustion of the spirit.

Effortlessly she dragged herself up off the lounger, feeling dizzy and disorientated as she stood up. She was on one of the layered roofs of the hotel, in an airy garden lush with potted palms and raised flowerbeds, with a sort of green felt carpet laid everywhere except for on the vivid blue tiling around the pool. As she stood in the sunshine, the heat hit her again, like a blast from a fire. After another dip in the pool she would have to go inside again—she felt weak from the heat.

The cool of the water closed over her like a blessing, and she sighed in pleasure. It was not crowded—just a few women, like her, lounging around the poolside. The hum of traffic from busy Orchard Street below could hardly be heard above the music piped out of speakers hidden in the greenery.

She dunked her head under the water, letting her hair

flow out like a mermaid's, floating back bonelessly, limbs splayed.

Eyes closed, she let the sun beat down on her face.

What am I doing here?

The question echoed around her brain, pointless, rhetorical.

She was there because Diego Saez wanted her to be there.

With him.

As she waded out of the pool, patting herself dry with one of the towels provided, wringing out her hair, she again felt the need to get back into the air-conditioned interior. Wrapping her sarong around her still damp bathing suit, she headed indoors.

She let herself into the suite with the key the reception desk had given her when she'd requested one, and stopped dead.

Diego was there.

He was sitting on one of the pair of sofas, legs extended, remote control in his hand as he watched stock prices flicker on the huge flat screen television in the room.

He looked up.

His face was shuttered.

But something flared deep in his eyes as they ran fleetingly over her scantily clad body, draped in the filmy sarong, dampened from the bathing suit beneath.

She stood there, incapable of speech.

She'd assumed—wrongly, it seemed—that he would be out all day—off downtown to the business section of Singapore, west of the harbour, where all the international banks and corporations were.

His voice, when he spoke, was dry.

'Did you sleep well?'

She swallowed, and nodded infinitesimally.

Inside her body, her heart suddenly seemed to have got too large. It was choking her. Her skin felt clammy, despite the chill of the room.

'Pleasantly rested?'

She gave that minute nod again, as her breath froze in her throat.

She could feel panic starting to mount, coursing into her bloodstream.

He got to his feet. It was a single, smooth, limbering movement.

She stood stock still, frozen to the spot.

He came towards her.

Her heart was racing. Like a stricken deer, fleeing for its life.

And finding itself at bay.

He reached a hand out. She tensed, her breath solidifying. He fingered the filmy material of the sarong.

'Very pretty. Have you been out shopping as well as enjoying the pool?'

She shook her head. He let his hand fall.

'You'd better go out this afternoon, then. You'll need clothes while we're here. Especially evening wear. There's a reception tonight. Buy whatever you think appropriate. Do you know Singapore?'

She shook her head again.

'Well, simply mention your preferred designers to the concierge, and they'll direct a car to take you. Obviously you will charge all purchases to me. Do you want a personal shopper?'

This time she managed to answer.

'No—no, thank you.'

He nodded cursorily. His eyes were frowning now.

'Did you bring any jewellery?'

For a moment she wondered if he was being sarcastic, but then he was speaking again.

'Then make sure you buy a dress that goes with diamonds.'

Words blurted from her. 'You're not buying me jewellery!'

He gave a derisive smile.

'I don't need to, Portia. I've already bought *you*. And the family bank, of course—and the stately home to go with it. You sold yourself to me, remember? Speaking of which...'

He reached forward again and flicked loose her sarong. It fluttered to the floor.

His dark eyes flickered over her. She felt as if she were naked. The damp swim suit outlined every curve of her body, clinging to her breasts, her stomach, outlining her pubis between the high-cut legs.

'Such a pity,' he said softly. 'I have an appointment with a government minister in forty minutes.'

He turned and walked away, back to his screen full of stock prices.

'Buy something—interesting—to wear tonight.'

She bolted for the sanctuary of her room.

CHAPTER NINE

THE car wound along a long, curving drive. On either side flambeaux flared, extravagantly lighting the way to a huge house set back in manicured grounds off the exclusive Tanglin Road. It was ablaze with light and people thronged within, visible through the acres of glass windows.

As always, as Portia stepped out of the limo, the heat of the tropics hit her after the air-conditioned cool of the car. Her high heels scrunched on the gravel as she lifted her long skirt minutely to make it easier to walk the short distance into the house. At her side the tall tuxedoed figure of Diego Saez kept pace.

The evening passed in a blur. The majority of people at the reception were Singaporeans, but there was a sizeable sprinkling of other nationalities, from European to African. She must have been introduced a hundred times, she realised, but she had taken almost nothing in. Apart from some of the younger European women, whose eyes openly speculated and who reached their own conclusions about what she was doing in Diego Saez's company, no one was interested in her. Diego Saez was the one they wanted to talk to. She was profoundly grateful.

Habit got her through the evening. She made polite chitchat, dutifully admired Singapore's achievements, talked a little about opera and art, and sipped at her champagne. Inside her the knot of tension tightened with every passing moment. She was continually aware of the dark presence at her side.

Dreading the moment when he would take her back to the hotel suite.

No, don't think. Don't think about that. Don't think about anything.

She took another mouthful of champagne.

Diego listened impassively as the chairman of one of Singapore's largest shipping companies commented on the growing cost of marine insurance. He was paying no attention whatsoever to the subject under discussion.

He didn't want to be here.

The fact that he had conducted a sizeable amount of profitable business already, with more in the offing, was of no interest.

Only one thing was of interest to him.

Getting Portia Lanchester back to his hotel suite.

She was wearing a long, classic-cut dress of deep blue. Had she done it deliberately? he wondered. Picked the colour he had first seen her in? She had dressed her hair the same way as well, in a tight French pleat that exposed the bones of her face, the line of her neck. The dress was high cut, very nearly a *cheongsam*, but with a round neckline, not a high standing collar. It was sleeveless, however, and every now and then his own sleeve would brush against her bare arm.

He could feel her tense whenever it happened.

He glanced at her profile. Her cheekbones were stark, her jaw set. Her skin looked ashen.

Around her neck, the diamond necklace he had hired for the evening looked garish. She had accepted it passively, making no comment as he fastened it around her neck before they set out. Only the sudden tensing of her whole body as he stood behind her had revealed her reaction to him.

Anger bit through him again. What the hell business had Portia Lanchester to flinch away from him like that? She had sold herself to him—and he had every intention of ensuring he got value for money from her.

And that included a willing woman in his bed.

He shifted his weight uncomfortably from one leg to the other. Thinking of bed and Portia Lanchester right now was not a good idea. It was close on forty-eight hours since he'd first had her, and it had simply whetted his appetite. He wanted her again—now—badly.

With scarcely contained frustration he tuned back into the conversation about global shipping.

At his side Portia Lanchester stood, stiff as a piece of wood, repeatedly sipping her champagne, her face a mask of tension.

All the way back to the hotel Portia leant into the corner of the back seat of the limo and stared out of the tinted window. Despite the hour, Singapore was still awake. People thronged the wide, litter-free pavements, tourists evident by their shorts and the cameras slung around their necks.

She looked out at them, dissociated, dispassionate.

She had drunk too much champagne, she knew. It creamed down her veins, flowing like an insulating blanket over her ragged nerves.

But she needed it. Needed something, anything, to keep her going.

To protect her through the ordeal that she knew awaited her.

Diego Saez would want to take her to bed again.

And when he did she would be unable to stop her body responding to him, catching fire, igniting with the flame he lit in her.

And she knew it would be a torment that would be unbearable.

But she would have to bear it. That was the very, very worst of all.

Don't think! Just don't think.

She went on staring out of the darkened car window.

When they walked inside the hotel everything seemed very far away. Unreal.

The swoop of the lift as it bore them upwards hollowed her out.

Cocooned in her haze of champagne, she walked into the suite and halted. What did he want her to do? Go into her room? His?

She stood, waiting for instructions. The room seemed to be moving in and out.

'Portia?'

Diego's voice seemed to be coming from very far away. She turned around to look at him and the room swirled around her.

She could see him looking at her, frowning.

'How much have you had to drink?'

She looked back at him. He was so tall, she thought, and those eyes were looking at her, making her feel faint and weak. His mouth had a sensual twist to it, for all it was set in a straight, tight line. The dinner jacket sat on his broad shoulders, superbly cut, the white of his shirt front strained across his broad chest.

She wanted to splay her hands across it. Feel the hard muscle beneath. Press up against him.

Weakness washed through her.

She gazed at him, drinking him in.

This was desire, she knew it. An emotion she had never before experienced.

Until Diego Saez.

She didn't know why fate had played so cruel a joke on her. Didn't know why of all the men in all the world it had to be this man—this man and only this man—who could do this to her. Reduce her to such weakness. Such desire.

But it was. And there was nothing she could do about it. Nothing at all.

Except yield to her desire, shed the frail armour she had tried to clothe herself in during the day, and give herself to the flame that he, and only he, could light within her.

So that she could burn for him.

It didn't matter that she would pay a price more terrible

than she could yet imagine for what she would have of him. And this was all she would have of him—this time, this brief time, when all he wanted of her was her body, though she wanted far, far more of him…

Slowly she walked towards him, swaying. Her whole being was focused on him. Nothing else existed any more.

He stood stock still. There was tension in every line of his body. His face was like stone. Except for one low pulse at his cheekbone.

The champagne creamed in her veins. How much had she had? She gave a slow, sensual smile.

'Just enough,' she whispered, and wound her arms around his neck and drew his mouth down to hers.

For one brief, rejecting second he resisted. Fighting for control.

But as the softness of her lips met his he was lost.

His mouth opened, opening hers with it.

He heard her sigh, felt her sink against him. Automaically he caught her body, holding her at her waist. Her breasts pressed upwards against him. His hands tightened on her waist.

Her mouth was honey. Honey and champagne. Nectar to his lips, his tongue. He kissed her deeply, consumingly, possessing her mouth, one hand sliding up her spine to mould her against him. The other slid down over her rounded bottom, pulling her into him.

His arousal was total, instant.

Waiting no longer, he twisted her round in his arms and lifted her up, then carried her through into his bedroom.

She was velvet and silk. The fine fall of her loosened hair was a pale swathe across the pillow. Her small, high breasts were tipped with coral, her white skin like pearl, flushed with the opalescence of desire. Around her throat the diamond necklace burned with blue fire in the lamplight.

On the floor, in a pool of sapphire, her dress lay discarded. Nearby his clothes were flung—carelessly, urgently.

He stroked her hair and tasted her mouth again, caressed the softness of her breasts, her slender flanks, the slim columns of her thighs. She arched beneath his hand like an arrow. He moved his body over hers, parting her thighs, honeying the dew from her, hearing the little moans she gave in her throat.

He wanted to fill her, sink deep within her, possess and spear the body spread wide for him, open and defenceless. He stroked her hair one last time, holding her wrists above her head, and entered her slowly, watching her face. Her eyes were open this time, denying him nothing, yielding him everything.

His control was absolute. This time he would set the pace, he would take her and enjoy her, watch her flood for him, helpless beneath him, pulsing for him, supremely vulnerable.

She came. He saw it happen. Saw the flush of her orgasm redden her breasts, sweep up along her throat, suffuse the lines of her cheeks. Her throat arched and a high, soundless cry came from it, parting her lips.

Triumph surged through him.

More than triumph.

But with a sense of cold, disbelieving shock he realised that he, too, was about to climax.

He could not stop himself. It surged through him—powerful, ruthless with its own need, its own urgency for satiation now, right *now*.

He climaxed in a single thrust, rearing over her, filling her, flooding her. The release was exquisite, and for a few timeless seconds nothing else existed. Then, as swiftly as it had happened, it ebbed away.

Exhaustion gripped him, and satiation—and something else that he could not recognise.

He didn't care.

His heart hammered, slumping in his chest, and he drew a long, harsh breath of relief. Relief—release—such as he had never known before.

For a few seconds longer he held himself over her. Then with a swift, withdrawing movement he disengaged. He did not look down at her.

For some reason—something he would not admit to himself—he did not want to look at her. Did not want to see the expression in her eyes.

Instead he rolled out of the bed and headed for the bathroom.

'The day is your own. I'm in meetings until the evening. What will you do? More shopping?' Diego's voice was clipped, almost curt.

'Why not?' Her voice was equable.

Indifferent.

She had her armour on. It kept the world away. Kept her inside a blank, numbing cocoon.

They were eating breakfast at a table set by the window. Portia was picking at a slice of papaya. Diego was polishing off Eggs Benedict. He seemed to eat with a huge appetite. But then he was a large man. Tall, broadly built. He would need feeding.

No, don't think about his body—what it does to yours…

That was for night-time. The night-time, when she had no armour to wear. When her naked body bared its aching vulnerability to his.

And he took total, ultimate advantage of it.

She pushed her plate aside.

A frown crossed his brow.

'Why aren't you eating?'

'I'm not hungry.' She reached for the coffee pot and poured out some more coffee.

Something flashed briefly in his eyes. It looked like anger, and she wondered why.

Diego watched her. She wasn't hungry. His mouth tightened. She would never have felt hungry in her life. She wouldn't know the meaning of the word.

He did.

He knew hunger, all right. Knew it like a dog gnawing at his guts.

He slammed the memory away. He would never feel hungry again—not unless he chose to.

He forked the last piece of the Eggs Benedict and sat back. He should be feeling relaxed, but he wasn't. Sex always relaxed him. And he had had a lot of sex last night. And more just now, on waking.

But he wasn't relaxed.

Maybe I'm going off her. Had enough of her.

His eyes flickered over her, sitting opposite him. She was wearing an emerald-green silk kimono, embroidered in gold. She must have bought it yesterday, when he'd sent her out to get the evening dress.

The wide sleeves made her hands seem smaller as she lifted her coffee cup with a graceful gesture, cupping it between her pale fingers. The emerald silk fell back slightly, revealing slender forearms.

As she lifted the cup to her lips the folds of the kimono shifted slightly, outlining her breasts at either side of the deep vee.

He felt his body stir faintly, despite its satiation.

No, he hadn't had enough of her.

Abruptly, he got to his feet. Whatever he might feel inclined to do, he had to make a move. He had a lot to get through today.

Suddenly the day ahead seemed very long. And tedious. He wanted it over.

Irritation nipped at him. Usually he enjoyed his pursuit of wealth, stalking new opportunities, harvesting existing ones. And here in the Far East there was a whole lot of both. Asia Pacific was wide open—the money to be made here was breathtaking.

He liked the attitude to money out here. It was open and

honest. These burgeoning economies wanted money—and they were prepared to work their backsides off for it.

The way he had.

But not everyone worked for their money.

He glanced down at the blonde head, bowed slightly as she drank her coffee.

Portia Lanchester thought she could stay rich just by offering him her body. Even though it meant soiling her lily-white hands on him…

A hard smile curved his mouth.

She wasn't so fastidious about him now. No lying back and thinking of her precious stately home! No, she shuddered with pleasure in his arms, her body pulsing, unable to stop her response to what he did to her.

His smile deepened, and there was a dark glitter in his eyes.

Making her take pleasure in what she was offering him was his own particular pleasure.

And shocking her with his demands—that added to his pleasure too.

He'd made a lot of those demands in the night.

And there'd be plenty more tonight, too.

But first he had to get through the day.

It stretched ahead of him endlessly.

I'm being a tourist, thought Portia. She had taken a taxi and gone down to the old centrepiece of Singapore, the wide green Padang, where British colonials had once played cricket in the days of Empire. Now the red-roofed cricket pavilion was dwarfed by the giant high-rise blocks that were modern Singapore. She'd seen the greystone Merlion, rising from the sea by the harbour, half-lion, half-fish, symbol of a city called into existence by Victorian merchants and now the busiest port in the world and a global financial powerhouse.

She was lunching at Raffles, the legendary hotel named after Singapore's founding father Sir Stamford Raffles, flanked by flat-leafed palms, gleaming white in its restoration as a tourist attraction. She sat at a table on the inner veranda, overlooking a pretty courtyard garden, picking at delicious food. She felt bad, because much of it would be wasted, but she could not force more of it down. She set it aside and went back to sipping her iced water.

She felt suspended. A fly in amber. Time was moving, but she was not. Her body ached, as if she'd done too strenuous a workout.

Inside her head pressure seemed to be building.

She knew, with a certainty that was like a knifeblade slicing through her, that what was happening to her was destroying her.

And there was nothing she could do about it.

She had become an addict, one who both craved and hated her addiction.

And her addiction was Diego Saez, who could take her to a paradise of the senses she had never known existed—and then abandon her.

She meant nothing to him. Nothing but a body.

Somewhere, very deep within her, a slow pulse throbbed. In her head the pressure swelled, seeking escape.

But there was no way out. No escape from what Diego Saez was doing to her.

She went on sipping her water, and staring out over the tropical plants of the central courtyard.

In the afternoon she went shopping, drifting through one mall after another along Orchard Street. She bought a few small items—some toiletries to keep her going, some underwear, a few more clothes, a handful of magazines and some books. She didn't know how long Diego Saez would be staying here in Singapore, or where he would go afterwards.

Or how long he would keep her.

She knew only that she had made her choice, and that from that choice there was no going back.

She would have to see it through to the bitter, bitter end. Whatever the price she was paying.

Diego lounged back against the pillows. A whisky glass was in his hand, and the sheet was half pulled up over him, riding low on his hips. In his lap, Portia's head rested, her fine silken hair spread over the curve of his thigh, her body stretched out across the wide expanse of the bed. Though he was spent, the pressure of her head on his groin was faintly pleasurable.

Idly he stroked her hair.

He took a sip of his whisky.

He felt—replete.

This time had been the best yet.

It was, he knew, because this time he had stayed in total control the whole time. There had been no more disastrous going over the edge at her first orgasm.

He had had to adopt several methods stay in control, but they had brought their own rewards.

Not least the satisfaction of seeing just how far—and how fast—he could extend Portia Lanchester's sexual repertoire.

And she was learning—oh, she was learning, all right. Learning just how infinite the pleasures of the flesh could be.

Tonight he had taught her just how much pleasure she could feel even without his possession of her.

She'd been reluctant at first, seeming to expect that he would want his own fulfilment, but he'd soon dissolved that away. It had not been long before she was giving those low little moans he liked to hear so much. He'd lain beside her, propped on one elbow, looking down at her, enjoying the way her nipples were like ripe red cherries. He'd brought them to fruition first, gently teasing and squeezing them, each upon each, until her breasts were a matched pair, each a swollen, rounded orb, their peaks suckled to ripeness.

Then he had let his hand glide further down, to tangle awhile in the tight curls at the clenched vee of her thighs, until, with another little moan, she had slackened and given him access. And there, touch by touch, stroke by stroke, he had teased her to pulsing, flooding readiness.

She had pleaded with him, gasping his name in her arousal as she never did otherwise, her breath shallow, her hands kneading supplicatingly into the sheets, eyes closed in inward focus on the sensations rippling exquisitely through her body. But he had ignored her pleas, only continuing with his task, his eyes half closed, merely dipping his head every now and then to suckle one breast or the other, keeping both at engorged ripeness.

He had felt the pressure rising in his own body, known that had he followed his own appetite he would have come down on her and taken his satiation. But he had resisted, letting his fingers and not his body arouse her, sometimes halting quite deliberately, so that her closed eyes had flown open, anguish in them, until he had laughed softly and continued. And with a long, sensual sigh her eyes had fluttered closed again and she had given herself to his caressing.

Only at the last, when the flush had already started to stain across her breasts, and his forefinger had poised over the quivering nub of her delicate aroused flesh, had he paused one final time.

Her eyes had flown open again, gazing up at him with imploring disbelief.

He had leant forward, kissing her languorously on the mouth.

'Tell me, Portia, would you like me to stop?'

A smile had played about his mouth.

Her expression had been worth every word of scorn and derision she had ever thrown at him.

She had been beyond speech. Only a low, agonised moan in her throat, and her hips straining upwards to try and catch his touch again.

'Well?'

There had been the merest exhalation of breath. He'd had to strain to hear it. But it had been enough.

'Please… Diego….'

He had smiled again.

'My pleasure, Portia. Or rather, yours...'

His finger had lowered to her, vibrating, and he had vatched her spill, the tide of her orgasm flowing out from hat one supremely sensate point of her being.

It had taken her a long, long time to come down from t.

He had made sure of that.

And then, and only then, had he sheathed himself and aken his own enjoyment.

He lay back now, supremely relaxed, still stroking her air. The second time, just now, had been even more plea-urable—and had shocked her even more.

Until, of course, she'd given herself to it and experi-nced, he was sure, a sensual banquet surpassing every ther.

He smiled reminiscently, taking another sip of whisky. 'he complex fiery flavour overlaid quite a different taste. 'ortia—the very heart of her.

His fingers trickled softly along the tender line of her eck and he felt her move minutely in response. The move-nent altered the pressure on his groin, and he felt himself tart to tighten.

After feasting on her he had given her subsequent or-asms in the traditional way—and himself. But now... He noved his hips a fraction and felt his arousal quicken. Now e felt in the mood for what he had given her.

He set down his whisky. He stroked her hair one more me, then brought both hands to cradle her head, turning gently inwards. She resisted a second, as if she did not now what he was doing, or why. Then, as he murmured her, at the same time sliding back the sheet, she finally eemed to realise his intent. Drawing up a little, to rest her eight across his now bare thighs, she dipped her head gain.

Diego sighed pleasurably, and relaxed back more deepl
into the pillows.

Her hair fell like a veil around him. Her lips were lik
velvet.

Portia took one more mouthful of the duck, and then se
down her chopsticks. The plate seemed very far away. S
did the gleaming white linen tablecloth, and the peopl
around the table.

Everything seemed far away. Remote.

Unreal.

'The duck is not to your taste? It is a speciality of th
house, but we can easily order something different for yo
if you prefer.'

The speaker, a petite, elegantly dressed Singaporea
woman, sounded concerned. Portia gave a slight shake o
her head.

'No, thank you. It's delicious. But I'm not very hungr
I'm afraid.'

Dark eyes narrowed at her from across the table. Sh
looked down at her plate, where the almost untouched duc
lay.

'Perhaps it is the heat,' said the woman. 'It takes a littl
while to acclimatise—especially the English. Your...
partner...' She hesitated fractionally, then went on, 'He i
more fortunate. You must be more used to higher temper
atures. Señor Saez?'

Diego moved his eyes from Portia to his hostess, the wif
of the president of an Asian telecoms company with who
he was discussing opportunities to invest in the developin
communications infrastructure of China.

'San Cristo is further north than Singapore, but, yes, th
summers are probably as hot as the climate here.'

'San Cristo?' said Mrs Ling politely.

'The capital of Maragua—one of the more inconspicuo
countries in Central America.' Diego's voice was dr

'Very little happens there to bring it to the attention of the rest of the world.'

'Wasn't there some turmoil there a year or two ago? Over elections?' Mr Ling enquired.

'Yes,' his guest conceded. 'A new popular front government was elected. It was not popular with everyone, however.' Diego's voice was even drier, but there was a grim tone lurking beneath.

Mr Ling gave a slight laugh. 'No, I would imagine not. Still—' he glanced across at his guest '—your interests, of course, Mr Saez, are global. And increasingly so.'

He went back to the topic of investment in China.

Portia reached for her cup of green tea. It was all she could face. The smell of the fragrant food made her feel ill. She took another sip of her tea and found that her hands were trembling. She tried to steady them, and could not.

She felt Diego's eyes on her, lancing at her.

'Are you all right?'

His deep voice cut through the miasma that was netting around her.

She looked at him. He was frowning.

'Perfectly, thank you.'

For a moment he held her eyes, and as he did so she began to feel pressure welling up inside her.

The expression on his face changed. He went back to talking to Mr Ling.

Mrs Ling made some remark to her about sightseeing in Singapore, and Portia forced herself to respond. But that same sense of dissociation started to float through her. Mrs Ling's voice seemed to drift in and out.

The pressure began to well up again inside Portia from very deep. Very slow, but inexorable.

She let her eyes rest on Diego. He was talking, completely absorbed in what he was saying to Mr Ling, who was listening attentively and nodding from time to time. As she looked at him she heard his words echo in her mind—*Not popular with everyone*… Heard the grim tone of his voice.

Nor popular with men like him. That was what he meant, she thought distantly. Maragua was probably one of those countries run by a dozen families, solely for their own interests, as their own personal fiefdom. They would resist any change of government, any threat to the power they wielded. When political changeover came men like him would pull out their capital and clear out, putting it somewhere much safer, like Swiss bank vaults and property in Mayfair.

Or invest it in telecoms in China.

With enough to spare for buying up ailing merchant banks and women who would not go to bed with them otherwise…

The pressure swelled in her head.

She set down her teacup and it clattered on the tiny saucer.

Mrs Ling paused in what she was saying. Portia had no idea what she had been talking about.

'Are you sure you are all right, Ms Lanchester? You seem a little—feverish.'

Portia forced herself to drag her eyes from Diego.

'I'm quite all right, thank you.' Her voice sounded clipped.

Across the table, Diego's eyes flickered over her.

There was a frown in them once more.

'I asked you if you were ill?'

There was a hectoring tone to his voice.

Portia turned away.

They were back in the hotel suite. Not answering, she walked across to the recessed section which housed the bar area, opening up the cabinet with its beautiful contemporary marquetry. She took out a bottle of gin and a tin of tonic, then opened up the concealed freezer to take out some ice, dropping a couple of cubes into a tumbler. The ice crackled as she poured the gin over it, and the tonic hissed and fizzed.

'Answer me!'

She took a sip of the drink, watching her hand shake slightly, and turned back to him. That strange, ballooning pressure that had swollen inside her in the restaurant had gone. It had disappeared as they'd come up here in the lift.

Something else had taken its place.

'Of course I'm not ill,' she answered.

'Then what the hell is wrong with you?'

She looked at him. The question was so unbelievable she could only stare at him.

'Portia—'

There was an odd note in his voice. She said nothing, only went on staring. He gave a rasp.

'Are you so incapable of speech?' he demanded.

She looked at him. From somewhere, she did not know where, the invisible armour slid over her.

'What would you like me to say?'

'What did you do today? Where did you go?'

She wondered why he was asking. What did he care what she did in the daytime? She only existed in the night-time. In his bed.

But she answered him all the same.

'I went to Sentosa.'

'Sentosa?' He looked taken aback.

'It's the island beach resort south of Singapore,' she answered indifferently. 'You get there by cable car from Mount Faber.'

'I know where it is! What did you go there for?' He seemed to be controlling his voice.

Her expression did not alter.

'To get away.'

His eyes narrowed.

'From what?'

From you. From this. To find, for a few brief hours, my sanity again.

She kept silent. It was all she had left.

She took another mouthful of her drink, and stood looking across at where he stood.

He was in a lounge suit tonight, the superb line of the tailoring moulding around his shoulders. She felt a kick go through her that was nothing to do with the gin.

And everything to do with her helpless, shameful addiction to him.

She wanted him.

Wanted to feel his body, hard and demanding against her.

Wanted him to strip the clothes from her and tumble her down on the bed.

Possess her.

Consume her, body and soul.

She took another mouthful of the gin and let her eyes wander over his tall, powerful frame.

His face darkened. He strode up to her, hands clamping around her upper arms.

She felt sexual excitement bolt through her. The sexual excitement he unleashed in her, night after night, that she had never known existed, that would never exist again once he had done with her.

He took the glass away from her, roughly setting it down. His eyes never left her. Something flared, deep in their depths.

'I don't want you drunk. I want you very, very sober…'

He pulled her against him, and lowered his head, spearing her hair with his hand.

And she was lost, sucked down into that vortex that sucked everything out of her. Everything except the consuming need to sate herself on him. And sate him with her naked, inflamed body.

'I need to speak to you.'

Portia's voice was clipped.

Diego looked up from the morning paper he was reading at the breakfast table.

Her face was expressionless. But then it always was.

Except in bed. Then and only then did that mask of indifference fall from her. Then, when he caressed her, possessed her, her face would show everything—everything that he was doing to her. She was helpless to resist her reaction to him.

He looked at her; his mouth tightened automatically whenever she had that face on her.

'So speak.'

A frown flickered in his eyes. Her face was looking almost gaunt. Her cheekbones were standing out and there was a stark look about her mouth.

She'd lost weight.

Her body was thinner, he could tell. It was hardly surprising. In the week they'd been here she'd eaten like a bird.

And it was starting to show.

She'd said she wasn't ill, so what the hell was wrong with her?

'How long are you planning to stay in Singapore?'

Her enquiry was cool, with that same edge of indifference that always got under his skin.

'Why do you ask? Do you think I've had enough of you yet?'

The skin seemed to tighten over her cheekbones.

'At the moment I'm taking unscheduled leave from my work. I need to know how much more I need to request.'

He laid down his newspaper

'Tell me, Portia, what if your request for more leave is turned down? What then?'

His eyes baited hers.

She didn't miss a beat.

'I would take unpaid leave. If necessary I would resign my job, effective immediately. Why do you ask?'

'To make sure,' he spelt out, 'that you understand the

terms and conditions of your presence here. You are with me until I say otherwise. Do you understand?'

For one long moment she looked at him. There was nothing in her eyes.

'You started this, Portia,' he said softly. 'And I promise you, I will finish it.'

He held her gaze a moment longer, then let it drop and went back to his paper, a tightness lashing inside him.

She reached for the coffee pot and poured herself another cup. As she set the pot back on its stand she found her hands were shaking again.

Kuala Lumpur, Manila, Taipei. The most prestigious hotels, the most luxurious suites. Days to herself, to do the round of the tourist spots, wander the shopping malls, sleep by the pool. Shut down her mind.

Endure.

And wait.

Wait for the night-time. Not the formal dinners or the business socialising that she did at Diego's side every night—poised, well-dressed, well-bred, with a flow of social chit-chat, trying not to drink too much, trying not to look at the tall, dark figure of the man of whose presence she was always, constantly aware. No, that was not what she waited for.

It was midnight. The midnight hours when she could finally sate her addiction for Diego Saez in what he did to her, what she let him do, what she felt in his arms, his bed. Addicted to his touch. Addicted to his possession.

It was a fever in her blood, in her body.

And it was burning her away.

Down to the bone.

Because, like every addict, she knew with a sick, hideous despair that there was a poison, destroying her.

But she had no choice. No choice.

Except to endure what he was doing to her.

* * *

Manila, Jakarta, Hong Kong.

He was pushing himself at a punishing pace. Something was driving him to it. He was doing business at a relentless speed, occupying every minute of the day.

Racing to get to the night.

When he could have Portia to himself again.

Not ringed around by other people, not with that cool, polite social smile pinned to her face, talking inanities because social convention demanded it, being that uptight, reserved, oh-so-English upper class female with her cut-glass accent and her *sang-froid*.

His mouth twisted. Cold blood?

Not when he had her under him, with the flush of her climax coursing through her! Not when she wound herself around him, feverish with desire.

Then—then her blood was hot…

That was the Portia he wanted—the one he got in the dark reaches of the night, when she belonged to him and him alone. When she yielded to him and him alone. When he feasted on her like a starving man.

Who could never have his fill of her.

He wanted her more with every day. His was a hunger that could not be sated, that grew with every passing day.

Consuming him.

Devouring him.

His mouth twisted into a savage, mocking smile.

How had it got like this?

How had Portia Lanchester reduced him to this?

Worse, how had he let it happen?

He did not know—knew only that soon, very soon now, he must find the strength to finish with her, sever her from his life.

Be free of her.

Before it was too late.

Portia leant on the balustrade of the balcony of a suite in a world-famous hotel in Kowloon, watching the *Star Ferry* ply its way across from Hong Kong island. The day was cloudy, the Peak wrapped in a white mist. She wondered what she would do today. She had already been sightseeing for three days. There wasn't much left of Hong Kong to see.

Perhaps she would go across to Macao, that strange, hybrid city, half-Chinese, half-Portuguese, with architecture to match. Or perhaps she would just stay here in this luxurious hotel.

The glass door slid open behind her.

'Portia?'

Diego's voice was brusque. She was used to it being so.

But as she turned and saw him standing there, hand splayed on the door's edge, those dark, hooded eyes resting on her, she felt, as she felt every time, the same surge of longing.

He met the hunger in her gaze and for a moment his eyes blazed with an answering hunger.

Then it was gone, blanked out with that familiar, shuttered look.

'Yes?' she answered enquiringly. Her voice was schooled to its usual level of steady indifference, which she always used when she had to talk to him.

He did not speak for a second or two, just went on looking at her with that closed expression on his face.

He looked tired, she thought, registering the observation with a sense of slight surprise. Though freshly shaved, and looking as superb as he always did in his hand-tailored business suits, the white shirt brilliant against the dark tan of his skin, his face looked drawn.

For an instant so brief she almost could not believe she had felt it, she had an urge to go to him, soothe her hand along his brow, wrap her arms around him to shelter him…

'I'm going to Shanghai for a few days.'

The curtness of his voice brought her back to reality.

She looked at him expressionlessly.

Again something that she could not read shifted in his eyes.

Shanghai, she thought. Would there be a tourist agenda there? It wasn't exactly a tourist hotspot, just an industrial and financial showcase for the new, expanding Chinese economy.

'You can go back to London.'

His words fell into the air.

She went on staring at him, her expression unchanging.

Again there was that movement in his eyes. She still could not read it.

'Did you hear me, Portia?'

'Yes.'

Her voice came from very far away.

'Your flight has been booked. A car will take you to the airport.'

She could only go on staring at him.

His mouth tightened.

'Portia—'

Her name hung in the air, and then without a word he slid the glass door shut and went inside.

She went on standing there, entirely, totally motionless. She could not see through the tinted glass of the balcony door. He had gone, disappeared from view.

For a long, long time she went on standing there.

When she finally lifted her hand from the balustrade to go indoors she found it was shaking.

CHAPTER TEN

HER flat was unchanged. Everything exactly as she had left it.

Yet she was completely changed. A different person.

As she set down her valise in the bedroom, her eyes caught her reflection in the looking glass on her dressing table. They slid away as quickly as possible, but not before she had seen the gaunt, thin figure in the glass.

She turned away, looking around her blankly.

She didn't know what to do.

Her mind did not seem to be working. She was still encased in the same deadening blanket that had surrounded her since she had walked back into the hotel room in Hong Kong from the balcony and realised that Diego had gone.

For want of something to do she went into the kitchen, running cold water and filling the kettle, staring about at the familiar units and appliances.

A cup of tea. That was what people had when they came back home after a journey. They had a cup of tea.

With immense effort she went through the motions of making tea in a mug with a teabag, then took it through into the sitting room. She switched on a table-lamp and sank back into the sofa. She felt so tired she thought she would never move again.

It was nearly midnight. The flight had deposited her at Heathrow some time after nine o'clock, but she had only been able to move in slow motion through the airport, and there had been a long queue for taxis.

She rested her head on the back of the sofa, shutting her eyes.

She wanted to feel something. Anything.

But all there was was that thick, deadening blanket, all around her.

She was home.

Home after a journey that had taken her far further than the other side of the world. A journey from which there could be no return.

She was no longer the person she had been.

Diego Saez had seen to that.

She felt that sense of pressure build up inside her again—the one she had become so familiar with. It seemed to balloon through her body, pressing outward. It threatened to break through, to explode her into fragments.

She clenched her fingers on the hot surface of the mug, willing the pressure to subside.

Suddenly, on impulse, she set aside her tea and stood up abruptly. With jerky, urgent steps she headed for the door, hurrying down to the bathroom. She stripped off her clothes, letting them fall, and yanked back the door of the shower, stepping inside.

The water rushed down over her, cold first, then warm, then finally hot. She reached for the soap and started to wash herself.

But she could not get clean.

Her doorbell went.

For an instant Portia froze, her hands hovering over the keyboard in the middle of the difficult—impossible—letter she was writing to Hugh. Then, pushing her chair back from her desk, she went into the hall from the second bedroom of the flat, which she used as a study. She opened the door into the outer hallway, which she shared with her brother's flat upstairs, and there was Tom, standing there, ready to ring again.

'Portia!'

He walked in.

'Where on earth have you been? You just about disappeared off the face of the earth?' He sounded both exasperated and anxious.

She was prepared for this. She had known Tom would realise she was home at some point and come calling. Though they did not live in each other's pockets, she did not usually vanish for such a long period merely on the strength of a brief message left on his voicemail.

'I took a holiday,' she said. 'It was all rather short notice.'

She did not look at him, merely led the way into the sitting room. It was hard to see him—very, very hard.

He followed her in.

'A holiday?' He was staring at her. 'Good God, sis, have you been ill? You look awful! Did you pick up one of those foreign bugs?'

She didn't answer him.

'Would you like a coffee? Or are you in a rush?' she asked instead.

He shook his head.

'I phoned Hugh to ask if he knew any more, and he said that all he'd got was a voicemail, same as you left me. Left late at night, too, like mine.'

'Yes, well, like I said, it was short notice.'

Tom was looking at her. She wished he wouldn't. There was concern in his eyes, worry.

'Portia, are you OK?'

She tensed.

'I'm fine,' she said automatically. Her voice sounded too brittle. But then her whole body felt brittle.

But she was functioning; that was the main thing. She had got up this morning, had gone out shopping to replenish her stores. It was a drizzly day—very English for summer. Quite normal. Everything was normal, in fact. The houses, the streets, the supermarket, the red London buses, the hurrying people. Quite normal.

Except that everything was happening through a thick, impenetrable, transparent glass wall.

Tom was behind the glass wall as well. She could see him, but he was very far away.

Or perhaps it was her who was very far away.

'You don't look fine,' he said bluntly. 'You look bloody. I think you should see the quack—get him to check you out. Some of those foreign bugs can be really nasty. Where did you say you went, anyway? Anywhere tropical? That's where the worst bugs are.'

'I'm fine,' she said again. Then, to get him to stop looking at her like that, she said abruptly, 'How are things over here?'

The moment she'd asked she wished she hadn't.

'OK,' he said. And then, expansively. 'In fact, never better. I've been given my "Get Out of Jail Free" card and I couldn't be happier! The takeover's forging ahead, and it's all a matter of paperwork now. Saez's man is in place, and he's just about running the show now—and I'm effectively on gardening leave. All I have to do is show up every now and then, just for appearances—I'm still a director, obviously, but I don't take decisions any more, thank God! Uncle Martin is out—pretty miffed, I can tell you. I got an earful from him about "jumped up foreign financiers"—you know what he's like! He rang a peal over me for my general incompetence and irresponsibility and went off in a huff. I don't care. He's not out of pocket, and he's still got all his non-exec directorships in the City to play with.

'You know,' he said, in a more serious voice, 'this takeover is the best thing that could have happened. It's extraordinarily fortunate that Saez thought it worth his while to bother with us.' He glanced at his sister. 'He's a seriously big wheel financially, you know. Still, maybe Loring Lanchester is just some sort of stepping stone for him—a lever to get to something else.' He shrugged. 'Who knows? I'm out of it now and I am just incredibly grateful.' His face sobered. 'I very nearly lost Salton. I came within a hair's breadth. Out of everything else that's all I care about—that Salton didn't go under the hammer. I've had a reprieve I didn't deserve, and by God, sis, I'm not going to mess things up again. I've managed to hang on to Salton, and now it will go on to my son.'

He rested his gaze on Portia, an almost sheepish expression on his face.

Waves of coldness were going through her. *A lever to get to something else…*

That was, indeed, all Loring Lanchester was to Diego Saez. A lever to get what he wanted—her in his bed.

The enormity of it made her faint.

Tom was talking again, behind that thick, transparent glass wall that still separated her from him.

'Speaking of which—son and heir and all that—I went to see Fliss this week. I've just come up from Salton now, actually, and it's all settled. We're not going to rush. Her mother wants a couple of months to buy her hat and all that malarkey, so it's likely to be September. In the meantime, I'm afraid I'm going to take advantage of this gardening leave and buzz off with Fliss somewhere. She deserves it—I've been a rat, letting her stew down there, not having the courage to tell her that with the bank about to crash I could never ask her to marry me. So I'm going to whisk her away somewhere really gorgeous. What's the Maldives like at this time of year? Is it the monsoon season now?'

He looked questioningly at Portia.

'I've no idea,' she managed to say.

'Oh, well, I dare say the travel agent will recommend somewhere suitable. Where did you go, by the way? Wherever it was we won't be going there! You've come home looking like a wet rag.' He frowned again. 'And you've lost weight too, Portia. You're thin as a bone! You really should see the doctor, you know.'

'I'm fine. Just jet-lagged.'

Her voice was short, but it was all she could manage. That pressure was building up again inside her head. She just wanted Tom to go—leave her alone—leave her inside her glass capsule.

But he wouldn't go.

'Jet-lag doesn't make you lose weight,' he retorted. 'You've got a bug, you know. You must have, because the only other reason girls lose weight is either because they're trying to catch a man or they've just been dumped by one. Neither is likely to apply to you, because I know there's been no one since you got so cut up over Geoffrey so—'

He broke off, staring at her.

She was holding herself together. It was hard, excruciatingly hard, because she was like a porcelain vase with hairline cracks running all over its surface. Inside the pressure was building up, and building up, and the cracks were widening…

'Oh, my God, sis,' said Tom in a hollow voice. 'Is that it? You ran off with some man and it all came to grief?'

He came towards her as if to take her hands, give her a comforting fraternal hug.

She stepped back. He mustn't touch her!

Or she would break.

The glass wall that was holding out the world, cocooning her inside it, would shatter.

And so would she.

'No! Don't! I'm quite all right, Tom. It—it wasn't anything serious. Just—just a fling.'

He shook his head, contradicting her.

'You don't do flings, Portia. So if some man persuaded you to go off with him there must have been something pretty deep going on for you.'

Yes, she thought, as the pressure ballooned inside her. I had to save Salton for you.

'He must have been pretty important to you,' Tom went on, his voice rich with sympathy.

'No! He wasn't important at all. He was no one.'

She could feel the cracks widening further. Any moment

now, the pressure would burst through them, shattering her into fragments.

He was still looking at her, pity on his face.

'I know how cut up you were over Geoffrey, and I've always hoped you'd find someone you could settle down with and marry and all that. I'm sorry this man wasn't it. Look,' he went awkwardly, 'you really do seem to have been badly hit by it, and although I know you're probably all set to go straight back to work, why don't you take a few extra days off and go down to Salton for a while? Mrs T would feed you up, and—'

'No!' The word shot from her like a bullet. 'I'm…I'm sorry, Tom, but I just want to be left alone. I…I can't go down to Salton.'

She could never go to Salton again. She had saved it for Tom, for his children, for his future with his wife, but the price she had paid meant she could never go there again.

Grief filled her, a huge welling up of grief. But she knew she could never go there again. She had exiled herself from it.

She turned away. She wanted Tom to go.

If he knew—if he knew what you've done! If he could see what you did with Diego Saez! If he could see what you let him do to you—night after night. And you craved it. You couldn't get enough of it. Couldn't get enough of him...

Her brother's voice came from very, very far away.

'I just want to be left alone, Tom,' she said in a thin, strained voice. 'I just want to be left alone.'

But being alone was no comfort. It was worse, far, far worse. Alone, by day and by night, she had to face her demon. The demon that tormented her,

Guilt.

Guilt for so much.

For giving her body to save Salton.

Guilt for having craved the man who'd bought it.

And, worst of all, pincering her with red-hot tongs, guilt at craving him still…

Because that was the worst, that was the ultimate guilt—that after all he had done to her she wanted him still.

The torment of it convulsed her. To want a man who had treated her like that. Who could take her, night after night, with nothing more than lust.

Memory flooded through her. Hot and humid and shaming.

Shaming because she had responded to him, trembled at his touch, burned beneath his skilled, remorseless caresses. A man who had blackmailed her into his bed because she would not come on any other terms.

But slowly, very slowly, out of the crushing burden of the guilt that pressed down upon her, another emotion began to stir.

Crushed long since by necessity. Repressed deep inside her. Because to give vent to it would be to lose the very thing she had sold herself for. An emotion that was so dangerous she had never once, not once, allowed it to surface. But it was there, like a slow, welling pressure, in the very core of her being.

And now it began to surface.

And as it did, as it made its relentless journey to the surface, she knew with a deep, abiding certainty that she must give it voice.

Or lose her mind.

Diego Saez sat back in a leather seat in the lavish chairman's office at Tencorp, an unreadable expression on his face. The chairman continued with his spiel, wondering whether he was catching his fish or not. With Saez you could not tell. What he did know was that if he did catch Saez for the joint venture he was proposing he would have caught himself a barracuda.

Across the room, on a wide black leather sofa, a third

figure was seated, the eyes in his narrow face flicking between his chairman and Diego Saez.

It hardly seemed yesterday that his chairman had despatched him to sound out Saez when he'd first appeared in London, yet in that time there had been a whirl of activity surrounding him. Piers Haddenham could have named half a dozen deals that had been set in motion between various City institutions and corporations, but the one that irritated him most of all was the Loring Lanchester takeover.

His mind flipped back to that bankers' dinner, and Saez looking over Tom Lanchester's iceberg sister. He hadn't shown his hand then as to whether it was the bank he was after or Portia Lanchester's frozen assets.

And all along it had been both.

Piers's mouth tightened. Typical of Diego's type to get them both—the bank and the cold-hearted bitch! Not that anyone knew about the latter—not here in London, anyway. If it hadn't been for someone he knew out in KL mentioning that Saez had turned up to a reception with the ice queen on his arm he'd never have known what was going down.

The meeting drew to a close.

Piers glanced at his chairman's face. He was not pleased, he knew. Saez was being evasive, and he'd brought up a whole load of time-wasting rubbish about insisting on running an environmental audit of Tencorp's proposal before signing up to any joint venture. It was just a tactic, obviously. Piers knew the deal being offered would make money hand over fist—what the hell were a few native settlements and some mangy animals in comparison with that level of profit to be made?

He watched Saez stand up and take his leave. As his gaze ran over the other man's tall, powerful frame, a familiar flush of envy went through him. The bastard had everything! Money, looks, and women throwing themselves at him. You'd have thought, mused Piers sourly, that he could have looked a bit more cheerful! As it was, his expression could have sunk a ship.

He stood dutifully aside to let Saez leave the office first, then followed him down the wide corridor towards the bank of executive lifts.

On the way down he attempted various pleasantries appropriate to the situation, but drew a blank response. As the lift doors sliced open, and they walked out into the huge, echoing lobby of the Tencorp reception area, Piers could not resist an unwise jibe. He felt like riling that self-contained bastard.

'So, turned up any golden nuggets in the empty coffers at Loring Lanchester?' he remarked.

His shaft got him nothing more than a silent look of unsmiling derision. Stung, Piers let fly another arrow. He hadn't sweated blood sucking up to this get-rich-quick merchant to get him to bite at the Tencorp proposal just so he could go back up to his chairman's office and get an earful about not having talked Saez out of that environmental audit garbage!

'Of course,' he went on smoothly, quickening his pace to keep up with Saez's long stride across the marble floor, 'you did get a personal sweetener, so I'm reliably informed. Tell me, was it worth buying a failing bank just to get inside Portia Lanchester's iron knickers—?'

He did not even see the fist coming. One moment he was taunting Diego Saez, the next he was sprawled flat on his back, blood pouring from his broken nose, hand clutching his dislocated jaw.

Without even pausing in his pace, Diego kept on walking to the door.

Rage consumed him. Cold, hard rage.

It snarled in him like an angry jaguar.

Not just at that loathsome piece of ordure he'd left groaning in agony on the floor.

At everything—the whole world.

But most particularly at two people.

Himself.

And Portia Lanchester.

His anger at himself was absolute. Unforgiving.

As he got into the chauffeur-driven car waiting for him at the entrance to Tencorp, his face darkened.

How could he—how *could* he be in this condition? How the hell had it happened?

He'd tried other women. They were never hard to come by. The ones he'd already had were always eager to come by for more, and every mixed-company social event he went to inevitably had a selection happy to make themselves available to him. Since returning from China and touching base with his European headquarters in Geneva he had deliberately run through half a dozen—old and new, in a variety of physical types—but every time, *every* time, he'd either sent them home or walked out himself.

They had done nothing for him. Nothing.

No woman did.

Only the memory of one.

Rage spurted in him again.

Why the *hell* did he still want Portia Lanchester? He'd had her—*Dios*, but he had had her!—so why the hell did he still want her?

Why was it only *her* body that he wanted beneath him, above him—any damn way so long as it was *her*?

Why was it only *her* face he kept seeing, by day and by night, intruding into business meetings, festering in his dreams?

How could he still want her?

A woman he despised. A woman who thought herself too good for his touch.

Except when his touch could save her family wealth…

Anger seethed in him.

How *could* he still want a woman like that?

* * *

The car pulled up in front of the Park Lane hotel. He would spend one night here, and then fly on to New York tomorrow. The Tencorp proposal he'd flown in to hear had been a waste of his time. They were not a company he wanted to do business with. Their environmental record was abysmal. He'd known it, but had stopped off in London all the same. It had been weakness to do so. He did not ask himself why it was a weakness he'd succumbed to.

It certainly didn't have anything to do with Loring Lanchester. The bank was being run now by someone who knew one end of a balance sheet from the other, and it might, given some proper management, be showing a decent profit by the time he sold it off to one of the multinational banking houses for a worthwhile price. He would not be out of pocket on Loring Lanchester.

Liar! The word mocked in his brain as he headed up to his suite.

Money was not the only currency in the world…

He walked into his suite and tossed his briefcase down on the coffee table. He needed a workout. Perhaps some heavy expenditure of muscle power in the hotel's health club would drain out some of the anger eating away at him.

More than just anger.

Frustration.

He was not used to going without sex for this long.

Three weeks since he'd got rid of Portia.

Three weeks of celibacy forced on him by his own crushing inability to summon the slightest interest in another woman.

How the hell long is this going to last?

How long before he was free of wanting Portia Lanchester?

With an impatient gesture he loosened his tie and headed into his bedroom.

The phone rang on the sideboard.

He picked it up as he went by.

'Yes?' he said curtly.

'I have Ms Lanchester in Reception, Mr Saez,' said the deferential voice of a hotel clerk.

He stopped dead. Had he heard right?

There was a long, long pause. The clerk at the other end waited politely.

Then, in a slow voice, Diego heard himself say, 'Tell her to come up.'

Déjà-vu, thought Portia, as she pressed the button for the penthouse floor. Or should that be *déjà-fait*? She wondered absently what the correct French would be for doing the same thing second time around.

But this time it was a very different thing she was doing.

The first time she had come up in this lift she'd been about to sell herself to a man.

This time—

Her mouth pressed into a tight, hard line.

This time a different transaction would take place.

The lift slowed and the doors sliced open. She stepped out into the quiet, hushed corridor. Diego Saez still had the same suite.

Definitely *déjà-vu*, she thought.

She hadn't known when he would be back in London. She'd kept a request open with Tom's secretary at the bank. She would, Portia knew, be able to find out from the new Saez-appointed chief executive's secretary when Diego Saez was passing through again.

The call had come this morning. Mr Saez, she had been informed, had an afternoon meeting scheduled, but nothing thereafter. Yes, he was booked into the same Park Lane hotel as last time.

Portia had dressed carefully. The business suit was freshly dry-cleaned, her court shoes newly polished. Her hair was drawn back into a French pleat. Her make-up was the bare minimum.

She knocked on the door.

It opened at the first touch, drawing back wide.

For one long, hideous moment she just stood, motionless, then with Herculean effort she stepped inside.

Diego Saez stood there.

His tall frame seemed to tower over her, his dark presence dominating her vision.

She felt weakness sweep through her, as if every bone in her body were incapable of holding her upright.

'Portia.' Diego's voice cut through her. 'How—unexpected.'

His voice was as deep as ever. But there was something else about it.

A jagged edge to the voice, leashed under tight control.

She didn't let herself look at his face, just looked past him as she walked forward slightly, moving into the room as he shut the door behind her. She heard it close with a final sound.

She clicked open her handbag and drew out a piece of paper, placed it down on the surface of the glass coffee table.

This time she looked at him.

His face was a mask, eyes like slivers of obsidian.

'This is for you,' she said in a steady voice. She clicked her handbag shut again.

She watched him pick up the paper, watched him register that it was a cheque, watched him register the sum it was made out for. And the payee.

He seemed to still. Then, expressionlessly, his eyes went from the cheque to her.

'And this is—?'

His voice was as expressionless as his face.

She looked at him. She was calm—completely calm.

Only somewhere very deep inside that bubble of pressure had started to build.

'For you,' she said. 'You were good. Very good indeed. I'm afraid I don't know what the market rate for stud services is, but I'm sure you'll agree that this sum represents a generous recompense for your time.'

She turned to go. A hand clamped down on her shoulder, hauling her back round again.

His face was a savage snarl.

'What the *hell* do you think you're playing at?'

She could feel that bubble of pressure rising inside her. It was starting to balloon through her.

'I'm paying you,' she spelt out, 'for the all the sex I got. There was such a lot of it, and it was so very—inventive. And certainly very educational.'

'*You* are paying *me*?'

She might have laughed out loud. Laughed at the expression on his face. It was outrage, anger, disbelief—and something more that she would not think about.

But she had no time to laugh. Nor inclination either. The feelings ballooning inside her made no room for laughter. No room for anything. Except its own swelling volume, which was growing inexorably, unstoppably.

His other hand closed over her shoulder, crushing her bones. The cheque fluttered to the ground.

'You *dare* to do this? You sell yourself to me like a whore and you then *dare* to offer *me* money?'

The pressure exploded through her.

Throwing up her hands, she pushed his arms away, stepping backwards.

'You bastard!' she cried out. 'What did I *ever* do to you for you to treat me the way you have? To do to me what you did? All I did was say no to you! Say no to going to bed with you! But you wouldn't take no for an answer, would you? You had to go on and on and on at me! Hunting me down because *you* wanted me and I didn't want you! And for that crime, the terrible, heinous crime of not wanting to go to bed with you, have the cheap, meaningless, sordid little affair that you wanted to have, for that *unforgivable* crime of saying no, you had to resort to blackmail! You played with my brother's *life* just to get me into your bed!'

His face was black as thunder. The rage was ripping through him.

'You came to me—offered yourself to bail him out!'

Her face contorted.

'I had no *choice*! You gave me no choice! You spelt it out in letters a mile high when you told me you might—*might*—buy Loring Lanchester! I got the message all right—you had to have what you'd been wanting from me or you wouldn't go ahead with the takeover! What choice did that give me? Tell me that! What did you think I would do? Do you think I would stand back and watch my brother lose Salton? Do you think I could have lived with myself if I hadn't paid the price you demanded? I did what I did for his sake. I didn't want to. Dear God in heaven, I didn't want to!' Her voice choked.

He laughed—a harsh, mocking sound that flayed her.

'No. You made that clear enough. You thought you were going to get away with lying back and thinking of your ancestral pile. You'd have kept your gloves on if you could—to stop yourself having to touch me!'

Her eyes were venomous with loathing.

'You're right. I would have. Your touch contaminated me. I didn't come to you a whore—but I left as one! You made sure of that! I had to take what you handed out or my brother's life would have been destroyed—but now, now I'm clearing my account with you! Not his! And *my* account is that cheque!'

'A million pounds?'

His voice was scathing, still black with anger.

'Why not? My body was worth even more to you! You bought Loring Lanchester just to force me into your bed! But a million is all I can raise in cash. It's nothing to you, of course. I know that, with all your money. And it galls me even to give you that, because if I think *I'm* privileged then it's nothing compared with you! Look in the mirror and tell me if you're proud of what you see! I might have been born with a silver spoon, but you were born with a golden one!

'God knows how much of your poor benighted country you own, how many wretched peons slave away for you on a pittance while you gad about the world on your merry way, making more and more obscene amounts of money—enough to buy banks as toys and buy sexual favours! So that's what that cheque is for. And you can cash it or tear it up or choke on it. I don't care! You bought Loring Lanchester, Mr Saez, but you didn't buy *me!* And now I'm rid of you!'

She turned away. Stumbling. Unseeing. The room whirled around her dizzyingly. Bile rose in her torn throat. She reached the door and pulled it open.

He watched her walk out. Standing stock still, every muscle frozen, immobile.

The door shut behind her.

CHAPTER ELEVEN

'THAT'S good, Jaime. Well done!'

Portia leant over the young boy's rickety desk, reading what he had written.

'Thank you, miss!'

A flashing white grin came her way, splitting the dark face looking up at her.

She smiled back. 'Now, copy the next sentence,' she said encouragingly, hoping she had got it right in her tentative Spanish. 'Maria, let's see what you've done so far.'

She moved on to the next child.

It was hot in the classroom, with not a trace of air-conditioning, not even an electric fan. But the children were used to the heat, and the money that keeping cool would cost was better spent on other things.

There was an ever-present need for money. For, however many children the refuge could take in, there were always more. They came from the punishingly poor slums of the city, where poverty and ill-health made their parents—if they had any—indifferent or incapable of caring for them. The refuge, Portia now knew, offered them the only chance most of them would ever have of getting off the streets, giving them some kind of education—some kind of hope for the future.

It had been a photo that had brought her here. An illustration in a charity fundraising leaflet that had arrived in the mail. It wasn't a charity she subscribed to, but mailing lists were passed around. This one had been from some kind of third world orphanage, or so it had seemed. She'd placed it in her in-tray. She would write out a cheque some time.

She had picked up the next envelope in the day's post, ready to slice it open with her paper knife. Her movements had been mechanical, unthinking, but doing something as banal as opening the post had kept her going.

It had been a week then, since she had confronted Diego Saez. A week since the venom had been drained from her in that maelstrom of emotion that had poured so unstoppably from her.

But it had not brought her any peace. How could it?

The old life she'd lived had gone for ever. She could not go back to it as if nothing had happened.

Diego Saez, what he had done to her, had changed her for ever.

Hugh, when he had received her painfully worded resignation, had been on the phone immediately, trying to argue her out of it. She had been terse, uncommunicative about her reasons, merely insisting that she would not be coming back to her job. The very idea of spending her days tracking down the identities of long-dead sitters for minor portraitists had seemed pointless.

But everything had seemed pointless. Nothing had had meaning.

Tom had taken Felicity off on holiday, and somehow she had bade them farewell. Somehow she had endured the other girl's open happiness, somehow she had reassured a still anxious Tom that she was perfectly all right and did not need to go to the doctor, despite being as thin as a rake.

But though her hands had not shaken any more, though she'd been functioning perfectly well, had been quite capable of going to the shops, cooking for herself, getting through the days, still she had been surrounded by that strange, muffling layer that kept the rest of the world very far away.

Until that charity brochure had arrived. As she'd slid her paper knife into the back of the next envelope in her hand her eyes had dropped to the photo on the leaflet again.

It had been a photo of a boy. Not more than twelve or

thirteen. Wearing a ragged pair of trousers, no shoes, a torn shirt. He was lying in a doorway, legs drawn up, head tucked in, arms wrapped around his body, asleep.

There had been something about it. Something that had made her want to stare. The photograph was grainy, she could not see the boy's face, only the long dark hair of his head. But there had been something about seeing him sleeping in that doorway that had made her look at the photo for a long time.

Then, putting down the envelope in her hands, and her paper knife, she had picked up the leaflet and opened it up.

It had been about a street children's charity in Latin America. An organisation dedicated to providing a home, shelter and safety for children who had none of those things. There had been more photos inside. Tiny children, dirty and barefoot, picking over a rubbish heap. A family cooking a meal outside a shanty, the mother's eyes dead, the children all painfully thin, staring blank-faced at the camera..

She had started to read. At the end there'd been a heading: *How you can help*. She'd placed the leaflet on her desk and opened the drawer to reach for her chequebook. She wouldn't be able to give now the way she'd used to, but she would still give something.

She had thought of the money she'd paid to Diego Saez. It had come from her private income and her shares, sold off despite the shocked protests of her broker, who had advised her strongly that this was not a good time to sell, and in such quantities, subject to such punitive taxation.

'I want to raise a million pounds cash, immediately,' she had told him, and hung up.

A million pounds for sex.

An obscene amount to pay.

But it had been the only way to lance the poison in her veins.

Poison he had injected there.

She'd given a bitter smile. He had so much—and now

he had a million pounds more. Another handful of gold on his towering heap. While children like those lived in filth and hunger and homelessness.

In the very country he had come from.

Maragua.

The charity rescued children from the streets of the capital, San Cristo.

Did he even know they existed? she had wondered, with bitterness in her soul. Their wretched lives were as alien to his lavish gilded existence as if he'd come from another planet.

Her eyes had dropped to the heading again: *How you can help.*

She had read on.

And as she had read she'd closed the drawer again.

And had reached for the phone to dial the number printed in the leaflet. A silent revenge on Diego's way of life...

Father Tomaso murmured grace, made the sign of a blessing, and sat himself down at the supper table. At all the tables in the room the seated children started to chatter as the eldest at each table dished out the food.

'So,' said Father Tomaso, addressing the adults around him, 'how are our latest crop of volunteers coming along? Have we made a good harvest this season?'

He smiled encouragingly. Though old, he was still vigorous, with a determination and a dogged dedication that inspired all his flock.

'Can you say that again in English, Father?' quipped a young man of twenty or so, in an American accent.

Many of the volunteers who supplemented the Maraguan house parents and teachers at the refuge came from America or Britain, and most were students, coming here in their vacations or gap years. Portia felt old in comparison—but never unwelcome.

She looked around her. The dining room was a plain whitewashed room, its plainness brightened by a vivid mual that ran around the four walls, painted by the children. t was a waving rainbow that wove in and out of an arkload of animals, some rather unlikely-looking from an anatomcal perspective, but all painted with enthusiasm and verve. Every child who came to the refuge added an animal.

This was their ark, thought Portia. Their shelter from the torm.

And mine too…

The storm had almost destroyed her. The storm that Diego Saez had unleashed over her life.

She would never recover. *Could* never recover.

Because although the anger and the guilt had gone, asuaged in that final excoriating denunciation of him, what emained was more agonising still.

A pain that would be with her all her life.

The pain of having fallen in love—despite everything he had done to her—with a man as ruthless as Diego Saez.

Father Tomaso was talking again.

'Tomorrow we have a visitor—a new volunteer! He cannot stay long, but while he is here I hope you will get good work out of him! He is strong, so I think we should corral him into helping with the building project. The walls of the new clinic grow high, but they must be higher yet, and there is still the roof to put on.'

'Who is he, Father?' asked one of the volunteers, curious.

'He is a most remarkable man,' answered the elderly priest. 'He lived here once, in this very home. He came here, half-starved from the streets, but he was not from San Cristo. He had come here from the country, a vagrant without family. With nothing. Yet now...' he paused. 'Now he has everything that money can buy.' Father Tomaso's dark eyes saddened. 'But nothing that it cannot.'

'He's rich, but he's going to work on our building site?' The volunteer asking the question sounded sceptical.

'He does not know it yet,' Father Tomaso remarked dryly.

There was some laughter.

'I have merely persuaded him at last to make an inspection of what his money is building—he does not yet know that his hands are going to make an equal contribution. In fact—' he paused again '—it will be a much greater one. For some, giving money is easy. For them, the real act of *caritas* is much harder.'

His eyes flickered over the table, resting briefly on Portia. She held his gaze minutely. He knew that, unlike the majority of volunteers, she came from a privileged background. But she knew he accepted that she had come here to battle her demons—demons that must shrink to insignificance compared with those that preyed on the lives of the children he rescued.

Portia's thoughts slid to the tale of the boy he had taken in, who had become so rich now. In her mind's eye she saw the photo that had brought her here, of the boy sleeping rough in a doorway.

She felt her heart squeeze with pity.

Father Tomaso went on.

'But, for all that, I am grateful for what his wealth can do. Thanks to him we can reach out to more and more who need our help—not just here in San Cristo but throughout Maragua and beyond, in other countries, for his generosity is great.' He gave a tired, defeated sigh. 'I only wish that he could find the time to come back and see what his money has done...'

'But you said he *is* coming back,' said someone.

'Yes.' The priest's eyes brightened, taking on a resolute gleam. 'Finally he has accepted my constant invitation. I must be glad he can spare the time—he is a man of great affairs now, with many calls upon his time, and he no longer lives in Maragua. Indeed,' he mused, 'I do not think he has been back here since he left to seek his fortune.'

'What changed his mind?' one of the house mothers asked.

'I do not know,' replied Father Tomaso simply. 'But—

His voice broke off suddenly, as an indignant squawk sounded from one of the children, followed by a voluble protest from his neighbour.

'José? Mateo? What is the matter?' Father Tomaso enquired.

As the children simultaneously vented their grievance—a dispute over the last piece of corn bread, resolved by sharing it—Portia resumed her meal. The spicy vegetable soup, with slices of sausage in it, was simple fare, but she ate it with appreciation out of the pottery bowl. An image slid across her mind, of herself pushing aside the gastronomic delicacies served up to her in one expensive restaurant after another across the Far East.

Memory opened its jaws and swallowed her.

She was there again, sitting opposite him, dressed in a gown the price of which could have clothed a score of refuge children for life, her eyes sucked to him without volition, without consent, but with a hunger that had ached within her like a famine.

A hunger that was still inside her.

That she would never sate again.

Why the hell had he said yes to the old man?

Diego swirled the brandy around in his glass and stared moodily across the hotel room. The hotel was new, and held no memories, but memories crowded all the same. He tried to banish them, but he could not.

They had invaded his mind since the moment he had stepped foot inside the first-class cabin of the plane that had brought him here across the Atlantic, on a journey he had never thought to make again. Never wanted to make.

But something had brought him back. After so many years, something had made him do what he had vowed never to do.

Go back to Maragua.

He had never gone back, not since he had slammed shut the door in Mercedes de Carvello's face. He had left the next day, never to return. Not even when the new popular democratic party, to whose funds he had so handsomely contributed, had swept to power. There had been no need for him to go back. He could invest his money in fair trade ventures and environmental projects, make his extensive charitable donations, as easily from Geneva or New York as from San Cristo.

So why was he back now? Because an elderly priest had invited him?

Father Tomaso had invited him a hundred times—and he had always refused. Had refused to read the reports Father Tomaso had sent him about what his donations were accomplishing. Had refused to do anything more than give what was easiest for him to give—his money.

So why had he said yes now?

He took a mouthful of the brandy. It burned as it slid down his throat.

So did the truth.

He lifted his head. Looked into the mirror that faced him across the room.

Words stung in his mind. Scathing. Scornful.

Look in the mirror and tell me if you're proud of what you see!

The taste of the brandy turned to gall in his mouth.

Guilt seared through him.

And something worse than guilt.

Loss. Loss of something he had never even had. Because he had never had her—never had the woman he had hunted down remorselessly, determined to possess her simply because he wanted her. And when his usual means had failed he had resorted to other methods—despicable ones.

And he had tried to justify himself for using them.

And that was the most bitter gall of all. There had been no justification for what he had done to her.

His mouth twisted. She thought him born with a golden spoon—one of the very kind he despised so much, who treated those like him as if they were trash, worked them to death, ran them down like dogs beneath the wheels of their fancy imported cars.

I thought she was like that—rotten and corrupt. Caring only for her money. Ready to sell herself to protect her wealth.

But she had sold herself to protect her brother—had paid for the privilege. A million pounds. Paid to claw back from him some shred of what he had stripped from her even as he had stripped the clothes from her body.

No! He mustn't think—mustn't think of that! Must not think of the worst, the very worst torment of all.

He looked into the face staring back at him and mocked it with a bitter, jeering look.

He had lost her for ever.

And his life had no meaning any more.

'Diego! What shall I say to you? The prodigal returns?'

The welcome in Father Tomaso's voice did not hide the dryness in it.

Diego cast a twisted smile down at the elderly priest. Father Tomaso had aged—that was not surprising—but he had not changed.

'Then you must allow me to pay for the fatted calf myself, Father,' he replied, matching his dryness.

'I'm sure you can make it tax-deductible,' came back the priest, his voice even dryer.

No, thought Diego, the old man had not changed.

Emotions churned in him. As he had got out of the car—despatching a visibly relieved chauffeur back to the rich side of town—they had assailed him, twisting like snakes inside him.

The past and the present slammed one into another. Memories into reality. Time collapsing in on itself.

He cast his glance around. The place looked just the same—the same brave flowers, assiduously watered, by the front door, the same white walls, the same brightly painted door.

And inside the same smell.

That hit him the hardest, making him pause in his long stride beside Father Tomaso's brisk pace.

The years dissolved.

It had been the smell that had hit him the first time Father Tomaso had brought him here, with hunger gnawing like a dog in his empty, hollow belly. It was the smell of food. Hot food. Spicy food.

It was there still. He felt saliva run into his mouth, as it had done over twenty years ago.

The priest did not pause, continuing his brisk and busy pace, leading the way out into the central courtyard. Diego followed him. They must be cooking the midday meal right now, for when lessons ended. He found his mouth twisting again as memory sliced beneath the skin.

He had fought against those lessons long and hard. He had not wanted to waste his time with letters, with numbers. Had only wanted, once his belly was full, to go back out into the streets again, away from all the relentless good cheer and pious charity. But Father Tomaso had spelt it out. No lessons, no home. No home, no food.

And besides, only cowards ran from what they feared, the priest had told him. And if it was ink on paper that he feared—well, then it was a shameful thing. For there were boys here, girls too, who were half his age and yet they were not afraid of ink on paper…

So he had endured the lessons. Endured the good cheer and the pious charity.

Neither had changed, it seemed. As he walked past the classroom block in the wake of Father Tomaso he heard a burst of laughter, childish and adult together, and then, from the next classroom, the sing-song chant of a prayer.

His eyes roved around. There was much more here now than when he had been living at the refuge. Everything was larger, with a second storey built on, and extensions. The plot size seemed doubled, too. He started to listen to the commentary that Father Tomaso was giving, indicating with swings of his arms what had been done with the money Diego had given.

They rounded the end of the classroom block. Another plot of land lay across the narrow road, and Diego saw a building site behind the perimeter wall.

'This is the clinic. It will serve not just the children, but their families and their neighbours. With the physicians and nurses you are paying for we can provide the more basic treatment. For anything more we must persuade them to go to that fancy hospital you have built for the city.'

'Tell me, Father,' said Diego, his voice still as dry as the priest's, 'would you rather I hadn't given the people of San Cristo a free hospital?'

The priest headed across the road, avoiding an old truck that jerked and jolted past him.

'I would rather you gave from your heart, not your wallet—the wallet you spend your life stuffing with more and yet more money! Your wallet is fat enough, Diego. But your heart—your heart is as thin as a starving boy.'

Emotion stabbed in Diego—it might be anger. Or something else.

He caught Father Tomaso's black sleeve and stayed him by the edge of the road.

'My wallet pays for this! It pays for a hundred places like this!' He swept his arm around. 'It pays for a hospital in the city, and in half a dozen other towns in Maragua. It pays to stop our forests being logged to the ground, our rivers poisoned with pollution. It pays for farmers to buy the machinery they need, for village tradesmen to buy their stock. Its weight even helps to remind our esteemed president that he would be *unwise* to listen overmuch to the self-pitying whines of those who think the taxes they pay are wasted on running schools to educate peasants who have no function other than to slave in their factories and on their *estancias* and ranches!'

Old eyes looked up into his, saddened.

'You have come so far, Diego. So very far. You have

achieved so much. The world is yours. So why, then, is your face as gaunt as an old man's, your eyes like a hunted animal's?' He paused, his gaze questioning. 'Why have you come back, Diego? Why now? Why have you stepped aside, even momentarily, from your gilded, glittering life?'

Heat beat down on Diego's head. The air was perfumed with the exhaust of the jolting truck. He let go of Father Tomaso's cassock sleeve and looked away. There was stone inside him, as heavy as the blocks of concrete neatly stacked inside what would become the gateway of the clinic his money was building.

'So,' he asked, gesturing at the site, 'when will it be operational?'

'Well, that depends,' said the priest, the dry note back in his voice, 'on how much labour is available. Fortunately, for today at least, we have an extra labourer to hand.'

He looked blandly at the man beside him, who could count his wealth in billions.

'I am glad to see, my son, that those doubtless extortionately-priced health clubs you belong to all over the world have kept you fit. Now, give me your jacket and tie, and those fancy gold cufflinks, and that watch that tells you the time in every time zone you are making money in, and off you go. The others will tell you what to do.'

Diego stared at him, disbelieving what he had just heard, the bland expression on the old priest's face.

'Do you not think it a shameful thing,' murmured Father Tomaso softly, 'to be a grown man afraid of honest labour when there are children here who are not afraid of it?'

He nodded at the building site, at a relay of children passing roofing tiles along a chain, grinning and shouting to each other as they did so.

For a moment longer he held the younger man's eyes, and then grimly, mouth tight, Diego Saez took off his hand-made jacket and his silk tie, removed his gold cufflinks and gold watch and silently handed them to Father Tomaso.

The priest took them, that bland expression still on his

face. But beneath the blandness his heart lifted for the first time since the boy whom he had once found sleeping in a doorway had arrived that morning, in his gleaming chauffeur-driven limousine. Diego Saez might be looking at him with a glare that could strip paint, but his eyes no longer looked like those of a hunted animal.

Merely an irate one.

As he watched his former charge stride onto the building site, rolling up the sleeves of his immaculate white shirt, he hoped he had done the right thing. Salvation was never easy—but if ever a man was in need of it, it was Diego Saez.

The devil was riding on his back.

Consuming his soul.

Diego strode up to the half-completed building. The chain of children stopped their relay and stared at him.

'Are you our new helper?' one of the boys asked him. 'Father Tomaso told us we would have one today.'

'Did he?' echoed Diego grimly. 'I might have guessed.'

A girl spoke up, maybe eleven or twelve.

'You look too rich to work. Your shoes are polished.'

'Don't worry—they'll soon get scuffed. Tell me, where do these tiles go?'

He picked up an armful, hunkering down on his haunches to do so.

'You take them round to the other side, where the grown-ups are working. Do not drop any—they cost good money,' the first boy warned him.

'I shall try not to,' answered Diego. He stood up, bracing his weight.

One of the younger boys was staring at him.

'You speak like us,' he said.

Diego stilled. He had answered them in their own street accents. He had not even realised he had done so. Had not even realised he still knew such patois.

He looked at the children. They were staring at him.

'I lived here once,' he said slowly.

Their stares of curiosity turned to open disbelief.

'But you're rich,' said the girl who had spoken.

'I was not rich when I lived here,' he answered.

Another child spoke.

'Father Tomaso says we are all rich. We eat every day and we have a bed to sleep in and clean clothes to wear. That makes us rich, he says.'

Diego looked at them, at their neatly cut hair, their bright eyes, not dulled now by hunger, or by alcohol, or solvents.

'Yes,' he said, nodding slowly. 'I think Father Tomaso is right.'

'He's always right—he tells us he is,' said the boy who had warned him against dropping any of the tiles. 'Are you going to take those tiles to where they are needed, or just stand with them all day? They all have to be moved today.'

'Whatever you say, boss,' said Diego, and set off with his load.

It did not seem to be as heavy as he had thought.

Portia heard the call for the midday meal—a wooden spoon being noisily banged on the back of an iron pot—and drew her lesson to its close. Dismissing the children with an adjuration to wash their hands before going into the dining room, she put away her well-worn teaching books and headed for her own small bedroom. She needed to freshen up and change her top—she was sticky with heat.

The volunteers' rooms were in a side block across the courtyard to the rear. As she emerged into the bright sunlight she blinked, momentarily blinded. When her eyes cleared she saw the morning shift of volunteers and children come across the roadway from the building site.

She blinked again.

And then froze.

Faintness drummed through her. Denial seared in her head.

No! This isn't true! It can't be!

Diego Saez was walking into the courtyard.

She felt her body sway and found herself clutching at the doorjamb. The breath was sucked from her body.

It can't be him! It can't be!

But it was—his height, his broad shoulders, his dark hair, his features. Him. Diego Saez.

Frozen, the blood draining from her, she leant motionless against the doorway.

Sweat was running down his back, soaking his shirt and his waistband. It was just as soaked at the front, and his hair was damp. Father Tomaso's dig about health clubs might have been accurate, but there was a definite difference between working out in an air-conditioned gym on top-of-the-range equipment and labouring on a sun-drenched, baking hot building site. Yet he wasn't about to complain. Not when he was working hard so to keep pace with a bunch of denim-clad students, some grizzled locals and a bunch of eager kids.

But by the time the signal to down tools was called he'd been ready for a break.

As he came into the courtyard—which, judging by the rusting basketball hoop on one of the walls, still served as the children's playground as well—he found himself wondering what other surprises Father Tomaso had up his sleeve for him.

His mood was strange. Overriding everything was a sense of physical depletion from two hours of unaccustomed labouring. But there was more than that. There was a sense, he knew, of cussed satisfaction that he had kept up with the other labourers. And there was more as well. There was a sense of satisfaction—completely alien to him—from working in harness with others, of his own free will, for something that was important.

The others were wary of him, he could see—the local hired workers were openly chary, and even the volunteers had been awkward about his presence at first. But there was nothing, he realised, like working with people on a task for breaking down barriers. Especially when some of them were children. Now, as he headed across the courtyard, he looked down to answer something that one of them was saying to him.

As he looked up again his eyes roamed around the buildings. Again that crushing sense of time collapsing in on itself came over him, of the past rushing up to collide with the present. For a second he felt the years dissolve, like copper sheet in acid, etching out the contours of the boy he'd once been, so long ago, in a different lifetime.

He could feel his heart thump in his body—and not just because of the physical labour he had done.

And then, as his gaze swept past the open door leading into the classrooms, it stopped altogether.

Portia Lanchester was standing in the doorway.

He stood rooted to the spot, and slowly, very slowly, lifted up his arm to wipe away the sweat running into his eyes.

He was seeing things. Hallucinations. Visions.

Memories.

Ghosts that haunted him, tormented him.

It could not be Portia. It could not. She was six thousand miles away, in that beautiful eighteenth-century house where she belonged. As distant from him as if she had been locked away behind glass—like a precious jewel that was forever beyond his reach.

Then, as he stared, he watched the figure in the doorway that looked so like Portia but could not be—*could* not be—turn and grope her way indoors and disappear.

And in that instant he moved.

She staggered back indoors. Dear God, it was him!

Not a vision, not a mirage. But Diego Saez. Here. Now.

Blindly she walked back down the corridor that ran alongside the row of classrooms. Her heart was pounding, her breath short.

Disbelief still flooded through her.

'Portia!'

She stopped dead.

It was his voice.

Harsh, demanding.

He said her name again, and this time it was not harsh, nor demanding, but strange—very strange.

As if he, too, were deluged by the flood of disbelief that was dissolving through her.

Slowly, very slowly, she turned.

And as she did so, her gaze fastening on him, she felt her heart squeezed in a giant vice.

'How can you be here?' he said.

His voice was strange, so very strange.

And yet so familiar.

She felt her knees begin to buckle and reached out a hand to steady herself against the wall.

She stared at him.

It was Diego Saez—but not Diego Saez.

He was jacketless, and his white shirt was smeared with terracotta dust. It was also soaked in sweat, and his hair was damp with sweat as well.

She stared, bewildered—bewildered by his appearance, by his presence.

And then into the silence came another noise—footsteps walking briskly.

Father Tomaso came around the corner.

When he saw the tableau in front of him he stopped dead.

Then, his eyes moving between the two frozen figures, he spoke, the blandness in his voice quite at odds with the keen, assessing look in his eye. 'Ah, Portia, let me introduce our latest, if somewhat temporary, volunteer. This is who I was telling you about last night.'

Breath hissed into her lungs and her eyes widened.

She dragged her eyes to the priest.

'It can't be! I know this man. He owns millions! He—he—'

'He used to live here,' said Father Tomaso simply.

She shook her head.

'No. It can't be true. It can't.'

'I found him in a doorway when he was twelve,' Father Tomaso said, his eyes never leaving her. 'He was sleeping. I had some food with me. He woke, sensing danger, perhaps smelling the food as well. I offered him the food but he would not take it. He ran, suspicious, wary. I watched him run. He had no shoes; his bones stood out with hunger. I found him again the next night, in another doorway. I offered him food again and told him I was simply a priest, no one to harm him. This time he ate the food I gave him—wolfed it down, tearing into it. And then he ran again. It took me weeks to bring him here, and he ran away several more times. But eventually, he stayed. Until...' He paused, and this time he glanced at Diego as well. 'Until he ran for the very last time. Out into the world he conquered.'

His eyes rested on Diego's face. 'But did you conquer the world, Diego? Or did it conquer you?'

Diego's face was set, as tense as steel. He did not answer.

Instead he turned away, making to go.

'Running away again, Diego?' came the voice behind him.

'No,' he answered, and his voice was harsh, self-mocking. 'Merely rejoining the ranks of the damned.'

'You're not damned, Diego.'

The priest spoke with a calm assurance that infuriated its target.

Diego turned back, a snarl on his face. 'What do you know about it? You stand there taunting me, but you know nothing. Ask *her* if I'm damned. Ask her!'

His voice was harsh, tearing from his throat.

The blood drained from Portia's face.

The light in Diego's eyes was vicious.

'Ask her what I did to her,' he said, his voice low.

The priest turned to Portia, studying her stricken face.

'Is he damned?' he asked her, almost conversationally.

Her eyes slid past the old priest, back to Diego Saez. Her heart was slumping in her chest, her breathing ragged. She stared at Diego's face. It was stark, pulled tight with tension.

It was him—and it was not him.

An image laid itself in her mind. The Diego she knew. Sleek, powerful, rich—reaching out for her to peel her clothes from her, lower her down beneath him on the bed…

Possessing her. Buying her.

Another image intruded. The photograph of the boy sleeping rough that had, for some reason she had never understood, so worked on her that she had walked away from everything she had once thought she had to come out here. A world away from all she knew. All she took for granted.

A world Diego Saez had destroyed for her.

The two images collided, then dissolved, one into another.

The man and the boy.

The vice around her heart squeezed unbearably.

Something poured into the space around her heart, filling it. An emotion so powerful she could not block it.

'Portia—' Diego said her name, his voice low, cracked. 'Don't look at me like that. *Por Dios!* Don't look at me like that! After everything I did to you I don't deserve your pity! Only your contempt!'

She couldn't speak. Could only slowly shake her head.

He closed his eyes, then opened them again.

'Don't make excuses for me. I did what I did to you knowingly—I thought you deserved it. I thought you were like—'

His voice broke off. Then, 'Like Mercedes de Carvello.' His voice was flat. His eyes dead. 'She was the wife of the man who owned the *estancia* I was born on—where my parents worked. They poisoned my father. She killed my mother. Ran her down like a dog in her sports car, when she was drunk. I accused her of murder and she had me thrown off the estate. I walked to San Cristo. Father Tomaso found me, living on the streets. Years later, a lifetime later, when I'd made money as I'd *vowed* I would do, I bought the *estancia* from Esteban de Carvello—he'd run through all his money. His wife came to me in my hotel room and offered herself to me—the son of her maid—to persuade me to let her go on living at the *estancia*. I threw her out.'

His voice shuddered to a halt. Then he spoke again.

'I thought you were like her—willingly giving yourself to protect your wealth. I thought your reluctance was because, like Mercedes de Carvello, you thought yourself too good for me—you didn't want to soil your hands on me. So I…I made you *want* to soil them…'

Faintness drummed through her.

Diego's voice came to her from very far away. 'They say that deeds bring their own justice. I can attest to that. I wanted you so much—wanted you for my bed. But you would not come. You thought yourself too good for me. So I gave you an…incentive.' He took another painful, ragged breath. 'But justice had been meted out to me—a terrible justice.' He fixed his eyes on her. They were dark and hollow. 'Content yourself, Portia, in your contempt for me, for what I did to you. What I thought you were. Content yourself and know that justice has been done. I have my punishment for what I did to you.'

He looked at her, his face like death.

'I fell in love with you, Portia. Fell in love with you, who can only loathe and hate and damn me for what I did to you. And every day, every day of my existence, I wake knowing that you hate me—can only ever hate me. All my life. That—' he let his eyes rest not on Portia but on the still face of Father Tomaso '—that is damnation. So whatever I do now with the rest of my life—here or anywhere else—it means nothing to me.' His face was shuttered. 'Nothing.'

He turned away.

A sound broke from Portia. A tight, broken cry.

Father Tomaso's eyes went to her.

Questioning.

'And now,' he said quietly, his eyes steady on her, 'it is up to you. You hold the key to his prison. Will you release him? Or keep him in his hell? The choice—' his voice was even quieter '—is yours.'

He started to walk away.

She wanted to call him back. Run after him. But he kept on going, and her feet would not move, her throat was paralysed.

She heard his voice toll in her brain.

The choice is yours.

Choice. She had had no choice. When Salton had been threatened, her brother's home threatened, she had had no choice. No choice but to do what she could—whatever it took—to save it. No choice but to accept the devil's bargain that Diego Saez had held out to her. No choice but to go to him. No choice but to let him peel the clothes from her and take from her what she had refused him. Refused because she would not be one more woman that he simply picked up, enjoyed, and discarded again, to move on to the next one.

And when he had peeled her clothes from her and taken her to his bed she had had no choice—no choice but to accept the shame, the coruscating, burning shame, of discovering so devastatingly, so annihilatingly, that Diego Saez—who was buying her, possessing her—could light in her a fire that she could not quench.

And when he had finally thrown her out, terminated that devil's bargain of his, she had had no choice but to endure the greatest shame of all.

She craved the man who had done this to her.

More than craved.

The silence stretched all around her. The sound of Father Tomaso's footsteps had ebbed away. Time had stilled to this one point.

The choice is yours…

The words tolled again in her brain.

She looked at Diego. He stood there still, turned away from her, shoulders hunched, hand splayed out on the door. He started to push it open, started to move forward.

The choice was hers. Now. Here.

To let him go. Let him live out the rest of his life damning himself, hating himself.

Or—

She thought of what he had been—that lost, wandering boy. Without family, without a home. With nothing. Not even shoes. Sleeping in doorways. Like the boy whose photo had brought her here.

Here. Now.

As he started to walk out she reached out a hand to him. It trembled as she did so. And as it touched his stained shirtsleeve he froze.

She took a step forward.

'Diego.'

Her voice was a husk. She could see the tension strapped along the lines of his shoulders, the curve of his back, outlining every muscle.

She spoke again. 'Diego—I—'

She couldn't go on. Her throat was choking, pulled so tight it was like a band around her breath.

She gave a tiny broken cry.

He turned. Faced her. Her hand dropped away from him and she just stood there.

Her eyes fastened to his and her throat worked.

His face was stark, emptied of everything.

His eyes were dead.

Her heart was crushed again in its vice.

She took a faltering step towards him. Holding out her hands to him.

Making her choice.

And as she did so the emotion that had flowed in around

her heart seemed to swell and flood, flood out all through her, like a great, cleansing wave. Washing everything away.

Her shame. Her guilt. Her anger. Her hatred.

She went to him. Wrapped hers arms around him, holding him so tight, so very tight against her, leaning her cheek against his dust-stained sweaty shirt.

For a moment, so long it felt like an eternity he stayed frozen, immobile. And then slowly, very slowly, she felt his arms come around her. Haltingly at first, and then suddenly with a desperation that crushed her to him, bands of steel fastening her against him.

She felt him shudder, the breath raking through his body. She held him tighter, and more tightly yet. How long she held him she did not know. Knew only that she would never let him go. Could never let him go.

She felt tears spill from her eyes. That high, broken sob came again.

'Portia! No—don't cry. Dear God, don't cry!'

But she cried all the more, an ocean of tears.

His arms around her loosened. Gentled. His hand slid up to her head, stroking her hair.

'Don't cry, Portia. Please don't cry.'

She lifted her head. Blindly, instinctively, she reached upward.

He could not stop himself.

He kissed her, taking her uplifted mouth, crushing her to him.

The heat of midday made her little room an oven. She didn't care. The fires of hell could have burnt around her and she would still have been in heaven. She smoothed the sweat-stained shirt from him, kissing his body. She felt him shudder.

She drew him down onto the narrow bed, her arms winding around him.

'Portia—' The hoarseness in his voice tore at her.

'I want you so much,' she told him. 'So much...'

The little bed could hardly hold them both. They did not care. With slow rapture they found each other's bodies. He spoke to her in Spanish—soft, wondering phrases that she only half understood, and yet she knew he had never spoken them before.

This was a new world for them both.

Only as he lay within her, and her body glowed like the sun, did he pause and tense, his voice grating as he gasped aloud, the words torn from him.

'I can't! I can't hold back—'

He surged within her and she arched to meet him, igniting at his flame, burning in the same golden purifying fire. An eternity of ecstasy.

Later, much later, they lay together in each other's arms.

For a long, long time they said nothing, only lay in the sheltering cradle of their embrace. Then slowly, haltingly, Diego spoke.

'You are my life, Portia. For all my life, you are my life. Whatever happens now, whatever my fate is to be, it is in your hands.'

She pressed her lips against his throat. A peace filled her—a peace she had never known.

'I love you,' she told him. And knew it was the truth. The only truth.

His arm tightened around her.

'After all I did to you?'

'It's gone now. Over. Washed away.' She lifted her head to look down at him. 'I understand now the demons that haunted you. Made you think me like that woman. And I'm not proud of what I did—but I didn't do it for myself. I swear to you I did it for my brother's sake. That's why I paid you that money—to buy back my self-respect.'

Her eyes clouded.

'I thought you worthless. Spoilt, arrogant, selfish. And I hated you. But I hated myself more—because I had fallen in love with you despite everything you had done to me. So I knew…' Her breath caught painfully. 'I knew I had to change my life completely. When I saw that photo in the charity leaflet, of the boy sleeping rough in a doorway, something about him caught at me so powerfully. And I knew then that this was what I must do. That it was the only way I could heal, find some meaning to my existence from then on. But I never dreamt—how could I?—that *you* could have been such a boy. I never dreamt, that I would find you here—the real you.'

A troubled look crossed his face.

'I am everything you thought me, Portia. Spoilt, arrogant and selfish. I am guilty of everything you accused me of. I wanted you—and I wanted you on my terms and for my purposes. I wanted—just as you said—one more fleeting affair, one more sexual indulgence of the kind I had filled my life with. But justice found me, Portia. Found me, punished me, and mocked me.'

He paused.

'I denied what was happening to me. Denied that I felt anything more for you than some kind of endless craving. But however much I had you, I wanted more, and still more. And I finally realised just how dangerous you were to me. Because I thought you a woman to despise—a woman like Mercedes de Carvello. So—so I ended it.'

His arm tightened around her shoulder, betraying his tension.

'I thought I'd ended it—but it hadn't finished with me. You went on echoing in me. I could not silence you. I reached for other women, but I could not touch them. I wanted only you. A woman who'd sold herself to me.'

He took a heavy, ragged breath.

'But I didn't care. I didn't care—I just wanted you. And I knew it was bad inside me—very bad—the day you came, throwing your cheque in my face. I had just smashed my fist into the face of a man who had insulted you. I knew then just how much danger I was in. Loving a woman who hated me.'

His eyes gazed unseeing at the low ceiling.

'Then you came calling, and held up to me a mirror that made me realise I had damned myself—and lost all hope of you. Lost all hope of everything. My life was as empty, as worthless as a dried husk. Then...' He paused. 'Then Father Tomaso got in touch, as he always does twice a year, to try and get me to come back here. I never had. Never. Not since the day I threw Mercedes de Carvello from my hotel room. But this time…this time I came back.'

She pressed her cheek against his chest, just holding him.

'You came home, Diego,' she said softly. 'And I was here, waiting for you—but I did not know it. Waiting for the real Diego Saez—not just the boy who slept rough in doorways, but the man now, who gives back so much of his wealth to those who still need it.'

He scooped her tight against him.

'They can have my wealth—but you—you, my Portia—you have my heart.'

'It's all I want,' she answered.

Salton lay bathed in sunlight. The honey stone was warm, with sunshine dazzling from the myriad windows.

Portia stood on the south lawn, Diego's arm around her. She leant into him, tilting her head so that her wide brimmed hat was not crushed. A happiness so profound that she could not measure it filled her completely.

There was no marquee. The late-summer weather was too fine. The wedding breakfast was laid out on tables in the dappled shade of the oak trees. She took a sip of champagne from the flute in her hand.

A vision in sunshine-yellow was making a beeline for her, champagne glass waving precariously.

'You see—I told you, didn't I?' an exuberant, if slightly inebriated Susie Winterton cried volubly as she came up to them. 'Didn't I just *tell* you that he was *exactly* what you needed?' She beamed up at Diego, standing so close to Portia. 'I told her, you know—straight after the opera! I told her you were just what the doctor had ordered—*and* I told her you'd marry her and whisk her away to your fantastic polo ranch in Argentina!'

She sighed romantically.

'It's Maragua, Susie. And it's in Central America, not South America,' said Portia.

'Wherever.' Her friend shrugged haphazardly, still beaming at them both as she took another mouthful of champagne.

'Nor is it a polo ranch,' pointed out Diego, with a twitch of his lips.

Susie was undeterred.

'I'm sure it's gorgeous, wherever it is and whatever it is, and I'm sure you'll be ecstatic and blissful and so ridiculously, wonderfully happy that people will stand up and applaud! And,' she added lavishly for good measure, 'you'll have gorgeous, adorable children! Lots and lots.'

Portia felt Diego's arm tighten around her.

'Yes,' he said, 'we'll have many, many children, Susie.'

'We've got a good few already,' added Portia. 'And there'll be many more to come.' There was a husk in her voice she could not hide.

Susie's eyes widened, confused.

'Diego's going to turn his *estancia* in Maragua into a children's home, Susie,' Portia explained. 'He already funds refuges for street children, but this will be a place out of the city, with clean air and no pollution and no slums.'

Admiration glowed in Susie's eyes.

'Oh, I think that's *wonderful*!' she enthused. She gave another romantic sigh. 'You've got it *all*, Portia! A man who's sex on legs, has got buckets of money and is generous as well. You've definitely, *definitely*, got it all.'

She reached to kiss Portia's cheek, and then, with a beneficent smile, Diego's as well. They watched her head off, and Portia leant her head deeper against Diego's shoulder.

'I *have* got it all,' she said. 'All—and so much more! More than I ever knew existed.

Diego's hand came up to tilt her face towards him.

'Then we are alike,' he said softly, brushing her lips with his, his eyes warm. 'For with you I have everything my heart can desire.'

For a long, timeless moment they gazed at one another, and then into their silent communion came the tap of a knife against a glass. A voice called for attention.

'The bride and groom!'

Glasses were raised, the toast drunk. Portia drank too. And standing on their own, beside the towering white wedding cake, her brother and his bride, resplendent in morning suit and yards of white satin and lace, accepted their toast.

Diego looked down at her, his eyes questioning.

'This should have been your wedding. This is where you belong.'

His voice sounded troubled.

She shook her head.

'I belong with you,' she said simply. 'Nowhere else. And I have had my wedding—and it was perfect. Perfect in every detail.'

As if it had been yesterday she saw again the tiny chapel at the refuge, saw herself walking down the narrow aisle wearing a wedding dress the teenage girls had made for her, and all the under-tens following behind her in a vast procession of flower girls and pageboys, until she reached the man waiting for her by the altar rail. As they had both knelt they had looked up into the wise eyes of the priest who was to marry them.

'You chose well,' he had said softly to Portia.

Tears pricked in her eyes now, at the memory. Yes, she had chosen well—for her heart had chosen, and her soul and body too. All the elements of her being. She looked up at Diego, the man she loved and who loved her. Despite everything that had happened.

Or because of it?

It did not matter.

All that mattered was that they had come through.

Come through to this state of perfect happiness, perfect understanding.

Perfect love.

He held her gaze, and her heart swelled and overflowed.

She slipped her hand into his and held it tight.

'The bride and groom,' said Diego softly, and lifted his glass—to his own bride.

His own true love.

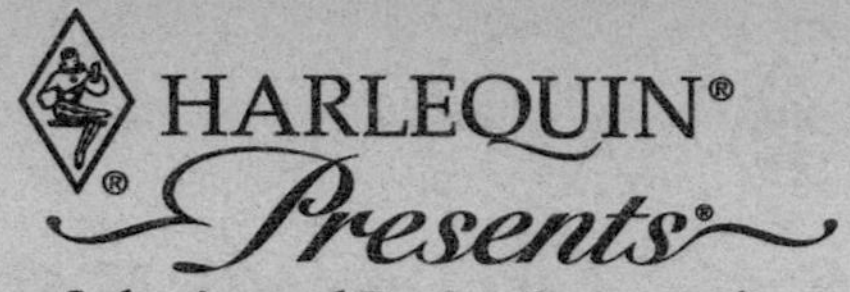
HARLEQUIN®
Presents®